In all the times she had listened to him play from her back porch stairs, she had never asked to join him. Perhaps that was his job.

"Rebecca." She was shrouded by the dark as he approached the back porch. He could see the white T-shirt she was wearing, but it was difficult to see much else with the roof blocking the light from the moon.

"Hi," she whispered, because the boys were in bed now.

He walked over to where she was sitting on the top porch step. "Come sit with me."

He held out his hand to her; even in the sparse light, he knew she could see it.

"No," she said. "I don't want to bother you."

"You're not bothering me." He reoffered his hand. "You're inspiring me."

After a second of thought, Rebecca slipped her hand into his. No matter how innocent the moment, it felt so good, so right, to hold Rebecca's hand. There was an instinct in him to find a way to hold on to her hand and never let it go. She slipped her hand free of his and fell in beside him, her arm brushing against his as they walked into the moonlight.

* * *

THE BRANDS OF MONTANA:
Wrangling their own happily-ever-afters!

Dear Reader,

I'm excited to recommend another Harlequin Special Edition book this month to encourage readers to discover the charm and appeal of these compelling contemporary romances. This series has always been a personal favorite. Many of the books feature Western settings, handsome cowboys, gutsy women and beautiful babies. The heroes and heroines are dynamic and relatable, trying their best to resist their attraction to each other while resolving the conflict that keeps them apart. These books will pull you in and take you on an emotional and satisfying journey. Each story ends with a marriage proposal or wedding—because the love and security of family is the ultimate promise of Special Edition.

The next author in this promotion is Joanna Sims. She has a unique and emotional voice that packs a real punch in 55,000 words. She structures her stories in ways that are sometimes unexpected but with deeply satisfying, family-focused conclusions that are realistic and true to the characters.

The Sergeant's Christmas Mission is the story of former army first sergeant Shane Brand and single mother and entrepreneur Rebecca Adams. Shane Brand lives with a lot of memories he wishes he could forget. When he meets Rebecca Adams and her two boys, Carson and Caleb, Shane embarks on a new mission: become the kind of man who deserves Rebecca's heart. Rebecca has a soft spot for men who have served their country, and it's easy for her to overlook Shane's rough edges. But when their friendship turns romantic, Rebecca discovers that Shane's past may be an insurmountable obstacle to their happily-ever-after.

Please take me up on this invitation to read a Harlequin Special Edition book and indulge in a heartwarming story. I do hope you enjoy the reading experience and will be back next month for another exciting book.

All the best,

Paula Eaud Miller

The Sergeant's Christmas Mission

Joanna Sims

HARLEQUIN® SPECIAL EDITION

Recycling programs
for this product may
not exist in your area.

ISBN-13: 978-1-335-46613-6

The Sergeant's Christmas Mission

Copyright © 2018 by Joanna Sims

Printed in U.S.A.

www.Harlequin.com

Joanna Sims is proud to pen contemporary romance for Harlequin Special Edition. Joanna's series, The Brands of Montana, features hardworking characters with hometown values. You are cordially invited to join the Brands of Montana as they wrangle their own happily-ever-afters. And, as always, Joanna welcomes you to visit her at her website, joannasimsromance.com.

Books by Joanna Sims

Harlequin Special Edition

The Brands of Montana

High Country Cowgirl
A Bride for Liam Brand
A Wedding to Remember
Thankful for You
Meet Me at the Chapel
High Country Baby
High Country Christmas
A Match Made in Montana

Marry Me, Mackenzie!
The One He's Been Looking For
A Baby for Christmas

Visit the Author Profile page
at Harlequin.com for more titles.

Dedicated to Tia and Alex...
Thank you for blessing our family
with my great-nephew, Shane Alexander.
I love you both.

Chapter One

A loud, urgent knock at the door and the barking response of his black German shepherd, Recon, awakened Shane Brand. He had passed out on the couch, as he always seemed to do, with a pile of crumpled, empty beer cans littering the coffee table and floor.

"Quiet." Shane ordered his canine companion to stop barking. Without any protest, the dog stopped barking and sat at attention, waiting for his next order.

"Man. Chill *out*!" the ex-sergeant hollered in a scratchy voice when the knocks kept on coming.

His tongue felt like sandpaper in his mouth and his eyes felt like they were glued shut. Damn, he felt lousier than usual.

Shane sat up, his head throbbing, wondering if he had any beer left over from the night before. After a couple of seconds of sitting on the edge of the couch, trying to assess the situation, trying to figure out whether or not he could stand without falling down, Shane stood up. He cringed at the ache in his back and neck, the stiffness in his left shoulder, from a night spent on his thrift-store couch.

"God bless," he muttered as he stretched his back. He felt like a bag of broken pieces hung together by rusty nails and screws.

More knocking.

"I'm coming, damn it!"

He kicked a couple of beer cans out of his path and shuffled his way from the small living room, through the galley kitchen, to the front door of his garage apartment. No one bothered to knock on his door—not his friends and certainly not his family. They'd all learned their lesson over time to let him come to them on his own terms, in his own time. Feeling annoyed and grouchy, Shane yanked open the door to give the person on the other side the death-stare. He was, unexpectedly, greeted by the loveliest wide-set, hazel eyes he'd ever seen in his life. He stared into those eyes, unable to look away, and something unexpected—something he couldn't explain—rocked him at his core.

"Hi," the woman at his door said.

Beyond her large hazel eyes, which were bright and clear, the woman's face was rounded, a little on the plump side, and the full lips were unsmiling. She looked tired and tense, and her eyes, now wary, were on Recon.

Shane took note of the two boys kneeling in the grassy courtyard between the main house and his garage apartment. This must be his new landlady; he heard the moving truck pull up, so he knew she had moved in. But he slept most days and played gigs in bars at night, which had allowed him, until now, to avoid her.

"He's friendly," he said of Recon as he leaned against the doorway, feeling light-headed and craving a beer.

The woman's curly light brown hair was pulled back into a haphazard bun at the nape of her neck, and she was petite, with a full bust and rounded hips. She was dressed for comfort in a faded Manchester Yankees baseball T-shirt, threadbare jeans and aqua-blue Chuck Taylors. Several ringlets of hair weren't long enough to be swept into the bun that framed her face; one ringlet had a Cheerio stuck in it. He almost reached out and plucked that Cheerio out of her hair but resisted the urge to do something so familiar with a stranger.

"You have a…" He nodded toward her hair. "A Cheerio in your hair."

"What?" With a half-frustrated, half-humored expression on her face, she reached up and felt around until she found the round piece of dry cereal and tossed it on the ground. "Thank you for telling me. It's been one of those mornings."

It had been *one of those mornings* for him, as well.

"I'm Rebecca." She extended her hand.

Shane took her hand, which seemed so small and fragile in his own, and was careful not to crush the delicate bones in her slender hand when he shook it. The women in his past always told him that he didn't know the strength of his own hands. For some reason, he wanted to be extra gentle with this woman.

"Shane," he introduced himself. "You the new owner?"

"We moved in Saturday," Rebecca said, her eyes

floating between his face and Recon. "I thought you might have heard the truck…"

He didn't respond as the new landlady glanced over his shoulder at the piles of dirty dishes in the sink. If he'd known the new owner was going to be knocking on his door so early in the morning, he would have tried to clean up the place a bit the night before. Shane stepped all the way outside, told Recon to stay put and pulled the door almost shut behind him. He had no doubt that Rebecca could smell the scent of marijuana mingled with the stale air of his apartment.

"Do I need to sign a new lease or are you giving me notice?" he asked. His previous landlady, Ginny Martin, had passed away and his lease had expired while her will was in probate. There was a shortage of housing in Bozeman, Montana; if he got kicked out of his apartment, he would most likely have to return to Sugar Creek Ranch, his family's cattle spread.

Rebecca, who held her body stiffly and had an anxious, worried look hovering in her eyes, glanced over her shoulder at her two boys before answering.

"I'm not here to kick you out," she told him. "I thought we'd see how it goes until the end of the month. Aunt Ginny always spoke so highly of you."

"All right." Shane nodded with a deadpan expression that didn't reflect his relief. Rebecca's aunt Ginny had recently passed away and left her historic home to her niece. Ginny's late husband had been an army man, which was partly why she'd had a soft spot for Shane. The feeling was mutual. Shane had been grateful to have a friend like Ginny and he missed her. It looked like, at least for now, Ginny was still looking out for him.

"I have to get my boys to school." She glanced at her phone to check the time. "We're running late. As usual."

"Ok. Well. Nice meetin' ya." Shane opened his door, about to walk back inside and get back to the business of finding a beer and lying back down on the couch, when Rebecca stopped him.

"Wait." She waved her hand at him. "This wasn't a social call."

Rebecca jogged over to the spot where her sons had been waiting for her, picked up the squirming kitten and headed his way with her two boys following along behind her.

Great, Shane thought. *I threw one back and four jumped into the boat.*

"We found this poor little kitten under the front porch this morning." Rebecca held up the wiggly, be-draggled kitten for him to see. "Is it yours?"

Shane got within three feet of the scraggly black-and-white kitten and started to sneeze.

"No." He shook his head. He had always been highly allergic.

"Then *we* can keep him," the younger of the two boys said to his mom.

"I'm sorry, Caleb," Rebecca said in a soft, but firm, tone. "We can't."

She handed the older boy the keys to the car. "Carson, you and your brother wait for me in the car. I'll be right there."

The kitten was making a high-pitched cry and Shane had a feeling the little creature was hungry, thirsty and missing its mom.

"I'm not sure what to do with him." Rebecca tried, unsuccessfully, to soothe the kitten. "I can't just lock him up in the house. I don't have a kitty box or food. Is there a shelter in town? Do you know?"

She talked so fast that Shane couldn't figure out when he was supposed to respond. That high-pitched crying noise was making his headache worse. While he was trying to figure out a solution to the problem, the kitten finally managed to twist out of Rebecca's hands; the moment it hit the ground, the kitten bolted through the crack in his front door, into his house.

"Oh!" Rebecca exclaimed. "I'm so sorry! I'll go get him."

The last thing he wanted was for his new landlady, who held the fate of his address in her hands, to venture into his dungeon. No one went in there and that's how he liked it.

"No." Shane blocked her path. "You're late. Get your boys to school. I'll catch the kitten."

"Catch?" She had turned away, paused and turned halfway back to him, the expression on her face concerned.

"Not in a mean way. I'm allergic." He tried to reassure her. "But I love all animals."

Rebecca hesitated for a moment longer, appearing to be conflicted. "Are you sure?"

"Yes." He frowned at her, not liking how distrustful she was of him. "I've got this."

She thanked him, seemingly relieved to have a solution for the kitten, and without glancing back at him, jogged toward the carport on the other side of the house.

Shane scratched his long beard with a yawn as he shut the front door of his house.

"Damn." The soldier stood in his galley kitchen, noticing, as if for the first time, how truly messy his small garage apartment had become. It was a dump. And it smelled.

On his way to the living room, Shane picked up the clothing and trash on the floor. If the kitten wanted to remain hidden in this disaster zone, he could do it. The first thing he really needed to do was get some light into the place. So Shane did something that he hadn't done in months—he opened the curtains and let the sunlight in.

Balls of dust were kicked up into the air when he yanked open the curtains. Coughing, Shane waved the air in front of his face. Dust was going up his nose and into his throat. After he got his coughing under control, Shane began the task of finding the kitten.

He'd always had horrible allergies, and now, with the dust stirred up and a kitten on the loose, he was sneezing one sneeze after another.

"Quit it!" Shane snapped, frustrated at his own nose. He grabbed a roll of toilet paper out of the bathroom, knowing that a box of tissues hadn't entered his apartment *ever*, and blew his nose every couple of minutes while he tried to find the kitten.

He searched the living room, picking up the trash as he went. The kitten wasn't there. Shane made a second cursory inspection of the tiny bathroom before he headed into his cramped bedroom. He tried to flip on the single overhead light, but then realized that the bulb had burned out sometime last month. Or maybe it was the month before that.

"Recon." He spoke to his companion. "You haven't seen a renegade kitten, have you?"

Shane tried to open the curtain covering the window in the bedroom. When it didn't move, he yanked a little too hard and the entire structure, curtain and curtain rod, crashed onto the ground at his feet.

More dust sprayed into the air, making Shane cough and sputter. "Damn it!"

This day was not going according to his usual plan. He should still be sleeping off his hangover, not worrying about a stowaway kitten.

Shane used a dirty T-shirt he found on the floor to wipe his eyes and his face. Then he balled up the T-shirt and threw it back down on the floor. Recon had lifted his head and was watching him curiously. That was when Shane noticed that his canine companion was harboring the kitten.

"Recon." The ex-soldier walked over to the side of the bed he rarely used. "Didn't I just ask you about this kitten?"

The kitten was curled up tightly in a ball between Recon's legs. The only way the kitten could have gotten up onto the bed was if Recon had put the kitten in his mouth like a chew toy and lifted him.

"Look, buddy. Don't get attached. You hear me?" Shane stared at the odd pair. "That kitten's not staying."

But, when he reached his hands out to the take the kitten from the safe haven, Recon growled. Recon *never* growled at him.

"What was that?" Shane asked, surprised. He pulled his hands back.

Recon rested his head on his paws, providing complete cover for the sleeping kitten.

The soldier stood by the bed, stumped by his dog's behavior. Recon was acting as if he was protecting a favored toy. Recon had always been friendly to cats and kids; he looked big and scary, but he was a sweet dog. But he'd never adopted a kitten before.

"Listen to me, Recon. I'm going to clean up and then I'm coming back for that kitten. So be prepared." Shane pointed his finger at Recon with a sneeze. "You can't keep him."

Rebecca had dropped her boys off at their new school, relieved that she got them there, with only minutes to spare, on time for the start of class. She had accidentally set her alarm for 7:00 p.m. instead of 7:00 *a.m.*, and she would probably still be asleep if Carson hadn't awakened her. She had kicked a large box of books in her rush to the kitchen—her toe was still throbbing—and then she'd dropped Cheerios all over the kitchen, and in her hair, when she couldn't get the new box open and overcompensated by yanking on the plastic too hard. She had managed to wrangle the boys, get them fed, make sure they were dressed and then trip on the way out the door, only to be greeted by a stray kitten problem.

In the school parking lot, Rebecca sat in her car, engine off, window rolled up, overcome with a feeling of emotional numbness and exhaustion. It had cost her a huge chunk of her profit of the sale of her house to move them from New Hampshire to Montana. She had adored Aunt Ginny, and her childhood memories of one magical summer spent at the Bozeman house had made her romanticize Montana for most of her adult life. So, when she learned that she had inherited the house, and things in New Hampshire had already unraveled after her divorce, a new start in Bozeman seemed like a promising idea. She had fantasized about how wonderful it would be while she packed her belongings and turned her early model Camry westward. But the reality of the house, which had fallen into disrepair, and the small college town that didn't seem to have many job openings for a hairstylist, made the move seem like a fool's errand. And so far, the boys hadn't come around to the idea that they were on a big adventure. They missed their home. They missed their school. They missed their friends. Most important, they missed their dad. What if she had just made a real mess of all of their lives by chasing a childhood dream?

One ding after another on her phone snapped her out of her thoughts and back into the present. The rapid-fire texts were from her younger sister, Kelly.

"Great," Rebecca muttered as she quickly read her sister's texts. Before she could respond, her sister called.

"Hey, Kell."

Her sister was a well-known Bozeman Realtor, owned her own company and genuinely believed that her sister was incapable of accomplishing anything in her life without guidance from her. Basically, Kelly thought that she was a screw-up and that moving her boys to Bozeman was yet another example of her bad judgment. Not that it was the only reason Rebecca wanted to succeed, but proving her sister *wrong* would be a bonus to making Bozeman work.

"Where have you been?" Kelly had her on speakerphone. "I've been texting all morning. Did you get the boys to school?"

"Yes, Mother," Rebecca said sarcastically.

"No good deed goes unpunished," Kelly said after a moment of silence. "I was just trying to make sure you got them to school on time. We both know you've always had a problem with being late."

Kelly had always been the "good daughter" and their mother had never let Rebecca forget it. She had been an A student, always on the honor roll, went straight to college after high school, married a sensible man after she graduated and then started her own business.

"Well." Rebecca turned the key to start the car. "The boys are in school and I have a ton of stuff to do, Kell. Thanks for checking on me."

Another pause.

"You're welcome," her sister said flatly.

They hung up and Rebecca headed home. As she always seemed to do after a conversation with Kelly, she litigated the conversation all over again, saying the things she *could have* said if only she had thought about it in the moment. She felt like she never really won a conversation with her sister. Kelly had been one of the major "cons" on the list when she had been contemplating living in her inheritance versus selling it and buying a little farm with some land in Manchester. It was a short drive back to the house that didn't feel at all like home.

Rebecca walked past her front door and headed to the garage apartment instead. All that was inside of the house was a bunch of unpacked boxes and wayward Cheerios; just thinking about unpacking all of those boxes and cleaning up the kitchen made her feel tired. Better to find a place for the kitten first and get that task off her mind.

Aunt Ginny's attorney, who had handled her aunt's estate, had only mentioned the positives of keeping Shane as a tenant—he always paid his rent on time, kept to himself, didn't have company always coming and going, and he helped out with the yard work and light maintenance of the home. She had never wanted to be a landlord—she didn't like confrontation, discussing money or dealing with fixing stuff that might go wrong. But the idea of having some extra income to handle monthly expenses made her realize that she didn't have a choice but to give the whole landlady thing a try.

The attorney did *not* mention that Shane Brand was a veteran with what appeared to be a shipload of issues. Right off the bat, she was going to have to address the elephant in the room: the garage apartment smelled like a marijuana factory. Why couldn't Shane Brand have been *easy* to handle?

With a sigh, Rebecca knocked on her tenant's door. First she would help the kitten, and then she would deal with the tenant problem. She wished she could make Caleb happy and keep the kitten. She just couldn't take responsibility for one more life. Not right now. Maybe later.

"Hey." Shane opened the door. He looked different— he'd taken a shower, and he was wearing clean clothes and shoes. His blue eyes, so much brighter than she remembered, were worried. "There's something wrong with the kitten."

She followed Shane to the back of the apartment, her mind naturally registering that Shane had cleaned up the small space quite a bit while she was gone with the boys. At the back of the garage apartment, in a room only big enough to fit a full-size mattress, Recon was on the unmade bed, whining and licking the kitten's head.

"He hasn't opened his eyes." Shane knelt down beside the bed.

She joined him, taking inventory of the kitten's condition. "How long has he been like this?"

"I don't know," he admitted. "I was cleaning up. I thought he was sleeping."

"Have you checked to make sure he's still breathing?"

She reached out her hand, but Shane stopped her.

"Recon is real protective of this little guy," the ex-soldier told her. "I checked. The kitten is breathing. Barely. I was just getting ready to take him to the vet."

"I'll go with you."

The kitten was listless but she could see that he was still faintly breathing.

"We're trying to help him, buddy," Shane said in a soothing tone to his dog. "You've got to let us help him."

When she first saw Recon, he'd made her nervous. He was a massive dog, all muscle and as black as a moonless night sky. But to see him protecting that tiny, helpless kitten touched her. He wasn't so scary after all.

Recon growled low and long in his throat when Shane reached for the kitten. For a tense moment, Rebecca actually thought that the German shepherd was going to bite his owner. She let out her breath, unaware that she had been holding it, after Recon let Shane pick up the kitten and wrap the little ball of fur in a towel.

Shane handed the kitten to her. "I'll drive," he said.

"Are you sober?" The question flew out of her mouth, which was unusual for her. She'd grown up with a father who tied-one-on every couple of weeks, and she could spot a hangover on someone from a mile away.

Shane opened the door for her and let her walk out first. "Yes."

"Sorry." She cradled the kitten in her arms. "I had to ask."

"I don't blame you." Shane pulled the door shut. "But I'm good."

They rushed out to his refurbished antique candy-apple-red Chevy truck. Recon took his position on the middle part of the bench seat and she climbed into the passenger side.

"What if they can't take us?" She rubbed the top of the kitten's head with her thumb, trying to comfort him.

"They will," he assured her. "I've known these folks for a long time."

It was a tense ride; she prayed all the way to the vet's office. Shane periodically glanced over at the kitten and repeated the same phrase, "Hang in there, little guy. We're almost there."

Chapter Two

Ever since he was a kid, Shane couldn't stand to see an animal suffer. He also hated to see Recon, who was still faithfully watching over the kitten, so worried and upset. They were lucky that Dr. Harlow could get them in after only a few minutes of waiting.

"I tried to give him water. He couldn't drink anything," Shane explained to the vet.

Dr. Harlow, a woman in her midfifties with frizzy, short salt-and-pepper hair gently handled the kitten.

"It's a she," the vet informed them. "When did you find her?"

"He's a girl?" Shane asked.

"*She's* a girl, yes." Dr. Harlow sent Shane the smallest of smiles.

"This morning," Rebecca told her. "Under my front porch. I have no idea how she got there. I didn't see a momma kitty or siblings anywhere."

"Unfortunately—" Dr. Harlow manipulated the kitten's belly "—she could have been dumped. Or her mother and siblings could have been killed."

"I thought of that." Rebecca frowned.

"She's severely dehydrated and malnourished. And she has an eye infection and an upper respiratory infection."

Shane instinctively put his hand on Recon's head, as much to comfort himself as the dog.

"Will she survive?" he asked the vet.

Dr. Harlow's slow response to his question raised his level of anxiety. The kitten's survival wasn't guaranteed.

"I'd have to draw some blood to know what's going on with her liver and her kidneys. We can treat the dehydration and infections," the vet told them. "Other than that, I need the blood work."

"Can I ask," Rebecca asked with a concerned expression in her pretty hazel eyes, "how much would all of that cost? The fluids and antibiotics and the blood work?"

"I'd have to get the front desk to figure out a total for you…it could be as much as four hundred, five hundred dollars."

The minute the vet gave them the total, Rebecca's eyes started to tear up. Shane didn't know her, but he'd been in some financial binds in his life. He knew he was looking at a woman who wanted to help the little kitten but didn't have the funds. Shane looked down at Recon; the dog hadn't taken his eyes off the kitten on the exam table.

The room was silent for a moment while Shane thought about his next move. In the silence, the kitten opened her eyes, stared up at him and made the most pitiful little high-pitched meow he'd ever heard. It was as if she was pleading with him to save her life.

"Do whatever you need to do to save her life," Shane told the vet. "I'll take care of the bill."

"We'll be keeping her here for several days." The vet nodded with a smile for him. "I'll call you then, Shane, with the results of the blood work? We'll talk about next steps then."

"Okay."

Dr. Harlow gently picked up the kitten and handed her to an awaiting technician. "Does she have a name?"

The ex-soldier didn't know how he'd managed to acquire a kitten, but that's what had happened.

Shane looked at Recon, who looked back at him with an anxious whine.

"Her name is Top." He sneezed. "Top Brand."

Rebecca opened the front door of her inherited two-story home and surveyed the work. What she really wanted to do was curl up on the couch to take a nap. But to get to the couch, she would have to create a path through the boxes. And as good as a nap sounded, she had to push herself to make progress on the unpacking while her boys were at school. Once they got home, there would be dinner to make and homework to check. Rebecca knew that this was a big adjustment for Carson and Caleb; the sooner she got this house feeling like a home, the better it would be for them.

"No rest for the weary." She tossed her keys on the kitchen counter on her way to find the vacuum. The cereal explosion she had created was the first on her list of chores.

"What a mess." She sighed as she leaned over to plug in her vacuum. The first outlet didn't seem to work, so she went in search of another outlet nearby. The third outlet worked, but now Rebecca was concerned about the fact that the other two hadn't.

"Oh, Aunt Ginny. What happened to your beautiful house?"

After vacuuming up the cereal, Rebecca avoided the boxes and headed to her sons' room instead. Carson had been a protective big brother from the moment Caleb was born; he always wanted to hold Caleb and feed him. The two boys grew up as best friends in part because they shared a room. Now that they could have their own rooms in this big old house, they still chose to stay together. Rebecca made the beds, something she usually had them do in the morning before school, and then grabbed the hamper and dirty towels out of the bathroom on the upstairs floor.

She disliked doing laundry, and the fact that she was picking this chore over the boxes was a testament to her hatred of unpacking moving boxes.

"You know what you need to do, Rebecca?" she said aloud as she used her back to push open the squeaky screen door leading to the back porch. "You need to get your butt inside and unpack those stinking boxes. Quit procrastinating!"

She put the laundry basket down on the stained concrete porch floor with a sigh, trying to avoid dwelling on all of the things that needed attention on the property. Luckily, Shane had maintained the grass and shrubs while the deed to the house was being transferred to her, but she had inherited the house and all of its many belongings. And some of those belongings were just junk that needed to be collected and hauled away, like the rusted, broken lawn chairs littering the back porch.

"I think Aunt Ginny, God rest her soul, may have turned into a bit of a hoarder," Rebecca mused as she loaded the washing machine.

When she went to retrieve the load of clothes she had washed the night before from the dryer, she found a ball of wet clothes that weren't dry at all.

"I didn't turn this on last night?"

She could have sworn that she had.

She turned on the dryer again and then went inside to begin tackling the boxes. With the trip to the veterinarian with the kitten, and her strategic avoidance, the day was frittering away. As she started opening the boxes labeled "Kitchen," Rebecca rehashed her interactions with Shane Brand. He was a bit of an enigma; his look was rough, with the beard and hair down to his shoulders, but there was something so soft and honest about his aqua-blue eyes. When they weren't red from lack of sleep and too much alcohol, she imagined that those eyes could make any woman take a second and third look.

For her, when she looked into his eyes, there had been a spark of familiarity somewhere deep inside of her that had flickered. She recognized him even though she had never met him before. Every now and again, she met a new person and it felt as if they connected on a soul level, as if they had known each other all their lives. That's what it felt like with Shane; it felt as if she had known him all her life. And the way he took charge in the vet's office and the mercy he showed that poor kitten put two additional points in the "plus" column to keep Shane on as a tenant. She had been so relieved when he stepped forward to help Top; now she didn't have to worry about breaking terrible news to Carson and Caleb when they got home from school. Now she could tell them that, because of Shane, Top had a fighting chance to survive.

Rebecca spent several hours unpacking the kitchen boxes, and when she was done, her back aching from bending over and her legs tired from climbing up on the footstool to reach the higher cabinets, she felt proud of herself. For the moment, she was just finding spots in the kitchen to blend her items with Aunt Ginny's. Eventually, she would have to thin out the stuff jammed into the drawers and cabinets. There had been many moments when Rebecca came across a favored bowl of her aunt's, something that stirred a childhood memory. It was in those times that she missed her dear aunt the most.

With two more hours of work time left before she had to leave to pick up Carson and Caleb, Rebecca grabbed a piece of cheese and an apple from the refrigerator and downed a bottle of water before she headed out to the back porch. She was feeling good as she stepped outside; the sun was shining and it took the chill off the early-Spring temperature.

"What in the world?"

The clothes in the dryer were still in a damp ball and were starting to have a faint odor of mildew. This time, she *knew* that she had turned on the dryer. The darn thing was broken.

She threw her hands up in the air. "Doesn't anything in this stupid house *work*?"

She fiddled with the dryer, pushing buttons, and then turned it back on. It sounded like it was working, but it wasn't. Frustrated, Rebecca kicked the dryer, but instead of hurting the dryer, she hurt her foot. In response to the injury to her foot, she began shaking the dryer in frustration. Slightly out of breath from the exertion of fighting with the household appliance, Rebecca stood quietly, hands on hips, feeling better for having told the dryer a thing or two. This day had been a mixed bag, and it was only half over.

"Lord." Rebecca pulled the ball of damp clothes out of the dryer and dumped them into the laundry basket. "I deserve a glass of wine. I really do."

After the trip to the vet, Shane and Recon took a nap together on the bed. It had taken some doing to get the dog to leave the kitten; he'd never seen Recon behave this way before, but there was no accounting for love, he supposed. Recon loved that kitten and that was the end of the discussion.

"Let's go outside, buddy." Shane grabbed a beer out of the refrigerator, feeling like his daily routine, which had been disrupted by Rebecca with the pretty eyes, was back on track. It was after noon and he was heading outside with a beer in one hand and the keys to his Indian Motorcycle in the other. He played music at night, slept the morning away and then worked on restoring his motorcycle in the late afternoon. That had been his routine for years, and that was how he liked it.

On his way to the detached garage, Shane heard Rebecca's voice drifting his way from the back porch. He didn't pay it any mind, determined not to get sidetracked, but a loud banging sound, as if she were getting in a fight with something, made him change directions, with a sigh, and head toward the back porch.

"You okay?"

Rebecca spun around at the sound of his voice. "The dryer isn't drying. I cleaned the vent. That didn't help."

Damn. So much for getting back to my routine.

He only used to see Ginny about once a week; he could tell that Rebecca was going to command much more of his attention and his time than her aunt had.

"Aunt Ginny always used to have a clothesline in the backyard," she said to him after she started the washing machine. "Any luck it's still around?"

"Let me take a look at it before you go to all that trouble."

Her pretty eyes widened in surprise at his offer and then she smiled at him. "Thank you."

Shane went to get his tools so he could open up the back of the dryer. On his way to the porch, he checked the air vent to make sure it wasn't blocked or an animal hadn't made a nest in it. Once he confirmed that the outside air vent was clear, he rejoined Rebecca on the porch.

"I really appreciate you trying to fix this for me," she said. "My sons make a ton of laundry."

"Boys tend to do that." Shane pulled the dryer from the wall.

"Yes, they do."

Before he opened the back of the dryer, Shane pulled the discharge line—the large silver tube hooking the dryer to the vent—out of the wall. "Well, here's some of the problem."

"Oh, my gosh." Rebecca peeked over his shoulder. "Is that all lint in there?"

"It's packed." Shane began to pull the tightly packed lint out of the line.

"You know, I had a brand-new front-loading washer and dryer, but I sold them because there was a washer and dryer listed in the will. I had no idea that they were the same washer and dryer that Aunt Ginny had when I was a kid."

"Your aunt liked to hang on to things, that's for sure." The memory of Ginny brought a brief smile to his face.

Shane sneezed several times, and once the discharge line was unclogged, he pulled some tissues out of his pants pocket and blew his nose. He was still sneezing from Top and his eyes were driving him nuts because they were so itchy.

"Is that from the lint or the kitten?"

He sneezed again. "I've never been allergic to lint."

"Shane."

"Yeah?"

"Have you seen your eyes?"

"No." He blew his nose again. "But they itch like crazy."

"They are swollen. And red."

"That explains it, then." Shane pushed the dryer sideways so he could remove the back.

"I'm going to get you some over-the-counter allergy medicine. I always have some on hand because of Carson."

"No need to bother." He knelt down by the dryer. Rebecca heard him, but ignored him. She disappeared into the house while he unscrewed the back of the dryer.

Once the back was off, Shane was sure he'd found a second cause of the problem. He had cleaned a large ball of lint out of the discharge line connection that was located inside of the dryer when Rebecca returned.

"That's *disgusting*," she exclaimed. "How has this dryer not caught on fire?"

"Luck."

"Here—take these. Generic Benadryl."

Shane decided just to go along with Rebecca; she had that motherly look on her face and he knew better than to fight those instincts.

"Thank you."

"You're welcome. Do you think the problem's fixed?"

"I'm thinking it is," he said while he unscrewed a second cover that connected to the lint. "But I want to check this first."

By the time Shane was finished, there was a large pile of lint, decades in the making, on the ground. He put the dryer back together, used a pair of her son's jeans as a test garment and turned it on. Rebecca stood next to him, her fingers threaded together as if she was praying for a miracle. Standing next to this woman made him feel strong for some inexplicable reason; she made him feel capable. How could a stranger make him feel like the Shane he was before his first tour to Iraq?

Shane took a step away from his new landlady, not wanting to feel anything, much less the loss of the man he could no longer be.

Rebecca didn't notice that he had moved away from her; instead, she was focused on the dryer. She opened the door and let out a happy noise, which signaled to Shane that he had successfully fixed the problem.

Rebecca turned to him with a broad smile on her face and her pretty eyes shining. She looked up at him as if he had done something amazing. He supposed for a woman with two boys and a basket full of dirty laundry, perhaps he had.

"Thank you, Shane."

He liked the way her two front teeth crossed just a little, drawing his attention to her full rosy lips.

He nodded and began to gather up his tools. When he stood upright, she was looking at him as if she had something to say. So, instead of turning to leave the porch, he waited.

"What you did for me today—helping with the kitten and now this—it means a lot to me."

"I always helped your aunt. I don't see any reason why I can't help you if you decide not to give me the boot."

"I think we could all share the space," she said, thoughtfully.

There was something she was hesitating to say to him—he could see it on her easy-to-read face.

"But there is something that is a deal breaker for me."

He waited for her to continue; his fingers tightened on the handle of the screwdriver, but other than that, he didn't show her how tense she was making him.

"I know that…" Another pause and a throat clear. "I know that cannabis is legal in some states now. But it's not legal in Montana."

Rebecca looked him straight in the eye then. "I won't have my boys exposed to anything illegal. Do we understand each other?"

His fingers loosened their death grip on the screwdriver's handle. "We do."

His response got a nod from her and she seemed satisfied with the exchange. He said goodbye then and walked down the porch stairs. Rebecca finished loading the dryer and the washing machine and then headed to the screen door, where she stopped and called after him. Shane stopped walking.

"Hey. I meant to ask you. Why did you name that kitten Top?"

Something twisted in his gut and he had to swallow several times before he said, "Because that's what I was. First Sargeant. My men all called me Top."

After she said goodbye to Shane, the rest of the afternoon flew by for Rebecca. She only had time to get a few more boxes opened and organized by room before it was time to pick Carson and Caleb up from school. Caleb had already started to make friends; he had always been more outgoing than his older brother. Carson, on the other hand, seemed to have a dark cloud over his head all the way home.

"I want to start riding the bus." Carson said his first words as they were pulling into the driveway.

"You do?"

"Yeah."

Rebecca worked to keep the sadness she was feeling from showing up on her face as she parked her car by the house and turned off the engine. Driving back and forth to school had always been their time together. She arranged her work schedule around the twice-a-day event.

"What about you, Caleb?"

Caleb grinned at her, making her smile at the space where his front tooth used to be. "I go where Carson goes."

She breathed in deeply and let it out slowly. "All right. I'll go to the office tomorrow and see what I have to do to get you on the bus."

They did their homework at the kitchen table, one of the only uncluttered areas, while she fixed dinner. The TV wouldn't be hooked up with cable until the next week, so the boys played video games after they all worked to clear the table, clean up the kitchen and do the dishes. She made sure both boys took their showers, brushed their teeth and then got into bed for the night before she poured herself a glass of her favorite wine. On the second glass, she remembered the laundry and went outside, onto the back porch. There, she was captivated by the sound of an acoustic guitar playing nearby. Quietly, she went down the steps and leaned forward to look around the corner. Sitting in front of the garage apartment, a single yellow light overhead, Shane was playing his guitar. There was a sad, compelling quality to his playing and it made her want to hear more. Rebecca quickly gathered up the warm, dry clothes out of the dryer, shoved them into the hamper and took them inside. A few minutes later, glass of wine in hand, she sat down on the bottom porch step and let Shane Brand serenade her with his guitar.

Chapter Three

"Hold on," Rebecca said to her eldest son. "Let me fix your tie."

"It's too tight," Carson complained, tugging at the necktie.

"Hold still and I'll fix it."

"I don't know why we have to go to church anyway. We never went before."

Rebecca frowned at the memory. One of the major causes of conflict between Rebecca and her ex-husband was faith. Her childhood had been turbulent and the one place where she had found solace was the church. Tim, her now-ex-husband, didn't have much faith in anything other than football and fishing.

"Well, we do now. This is a fresh start for us. Besides, church is a great place to meet new friends."

Carson grumbled something unintelligible and Rebecca just ignored it with a smile and a quick kiss on her eldest son's cheek. "You look so handsome in this suit."

"How do I look?" Caleb asked, his sweet cherub face turned up to her.

She leaned down and made kissing noises in his neck until he started to giggle. "Handsome."

Carson walked on one side of her and Caleb on the other, holding her hand. An older lady with short curly snow-white hair and a cotton floral dress greeted them at the doorway of the First Presbyterian Church.

"Welcome." The greeter gave them a friendly smile, along with a program. "It's always so nice to see new faces."

"Thank you." Rebecca returned the smile.

"Sit anywhere you'd like."

Rebecca chose to sit near the back of the church, wanting to get the lay of the land before moving forward. She had no idea if this was the right church for her; all she knew was that this move to Bozeman was going to give her a chance to reconnect with her childhood faith.

"Don't put your feet on the back of the pews." She stilled her youngest son's swinging legs.

She handed her phone to Caleb so he could play a game while they waited. She whispered, "Just until the service starts."

As the church filled with people, Rebecca found herself smiling with happiness that was bubbling up from the inside of her body. For the first time since she had taken the drastic step to move her family to Bozeman, she felt as if she were home. One of the last people to arrive at the church was a petite, slender redhead carrying a fair-skinned baby girl. The baby girl, who was dressed in a flouncy lace dress, had the widest, brightest blue eyes Rebecca had ever seen. The woman looked around and spotted an empty seat in the pew in front of them. The redhead made her way to the spot and sat down. Rebecca waved at the baby girl and the little girl reached out her chubby hand and then quickly ducked her head into her mother's shoulder.

Once the pastor began the service, his flock quieted. Rebecca was impressed with the sermon and she loved the singing. So many hymns that she had forgotten were jarred from the depths of her childhood memories when the choir sang. Carson half-heartedly joined the singing, but Caleb avidly followed along, singing off-key and loudly with her as she pointed to each word in the hymnal. After the choir finished its first set, the pastor asked that everyone present turn to a neighbor and shake hands. The redhead with the baby turned around and offered Rebecca her hand.

"Hi, there." The redhead had dark green eyes and a lovely oval face. "I'm Savannah. And this little sweet pea is Amanda."

"Rebecca Adams," she said. "And these are my boys, Carson and Caleb."

"Rebecca Adams," Savannah repeated. "Why does that name sound so familiar to me? Are you new to Bozeman?"

She nodded. "This is our first full week here. I inherited a house from my aunt and I thought, why not give Montana a chance."

"Oh. I'm so sorry for your loss." Savannah bounced Amanda a little to keep her smiling. "What was your aunt's name?"

"Ginger Martin. Everyone called her Ginny."

Savannah's expression lit up like a light bulb had just gone off in her head. "*That's* why your name is familiar. My brother-in-law is your tenant."

"Shane?"

Savannah nodded. "I'm married to his brother, Bruce."

"Small world."

"Small town."

The pastor brought everyone's attention back to the front of the church.

Savannah reached out and touched her arm. In a whisper she said, "We'll talk more after church."

At the end of the service, and against her harshly whispered words, Carson bolted out of the church with Caleb tagging behind. Savannah fell in beside her as they slowly milled out into the sweet afternoon sun-filled air.

"So, what did you think?" Savannah asked.

"About the service?"

A nod. "I hope you liked it. I'd love to have someone to sit with on Sundays; not that Amanda isn't great company."

"I couldn't believe how good she was; she didn't make a peep the whole time."

"I know. It's the strangest thing. She cries plenty the rest of the time. But during church service, not a peep."

"Well, I liked it. I want to come back."

"Oh, that's good news." Savannah stopped at the crosswalk. "Then let's sit together next Sunday."

"Okay." Rebecca felt heartened that she might have already met a potential friend in Savannah. Making a connection to the community was one of the reasons she had wanted to find a church to attend.

They waved goodbye and Savannah headed off in

the opposite direction. When she heard her name called, Rebecca turned around to see that Savannah was walking quickly toward her.

"A thought just hit me, and I felt like I needed to say this to you."

Rebecca waited for the words.

"I don't know if you were aware of the fact that Shane is a veteran."

"I am."

"He did a lot of tours." Savannah's expression reflected her concern when she spoke of her brother-in-law.

"My father was a Vietnam vet." Rebecca wanted to reassure her new acquaintance that she understood, on a deeper level, what it was like to live with a veteran who may not have returned from war the same as they had left.

"Then you understand."

"Yes. I really do."

"Well." Savannah ducked her head toward her and lowered her voice as if she was sharing a secret. "I know Shane can seem a bit off-putting, but I want you to know, that man truly has a heart of gold."

Shane had played a gig the night before and had slept off his hangover, so when he awakened on Sunday afternoon, he felt as if all had been set right in his world. He started his day by taking care of Recon's needs, which included a wrestling match on the floor. And then he cracked open a beer for brunch.

"Come on, buddy. Let's get some work done."

Recon followed him to the garage. He had managed to get his hands on a 1943 Indian 841, one of the one thousand that had been built to spec specifically for the

US Army during World War II. Shane didn't mind living in a small apartment because he could pour more of his money into restoring the vintage motorcycle.

Shane rolled the motorcycle out to the paved area right in front of his apartment. He'd been working on the restoration for several years. He had completely disassembled the bike, checked every part and then reassembled it. The motorcycle had also been restored to its original army camouflage green. He felt proud of his accomplishment, but also a little sad. Restoring this motorcycle had been his focus for years; what was he going to do with his time once the job was complete?

He was tinkering with a lug nut when Recon started barking at the sound of a car pulling in the driveway. He'd figured Rebecca and her boys were gone because it was quiet over at the main house.

"Stay." Shane gave the command to the dog. Recon whined a little, looked back at him, but sat down and stayed put.

The quiet he had been enjoying was interrupted by the sound of Carson and Caleb chasing each other up the driveway, their laughter, surprisingly, not annoying him all that much. The two boys ran toward the back of the house, but when they spotted Recon, they made a sharp right and headed his way. Recon wagged his tail and barked a greeting.

"Hey." Carson was wearing a suit, but the tie was draped around his neck, and he was barefoot, carrying his shoes and socks in his hand.

"Hi, guys," Shane responded.

"Hi." Caleb waved his hand in front of his body, like he was drawing a rainbow, and grinned at him, his head tilted to the side, squinting against the sunlight. "Can I pet Recon?"

"He's been waiting all day for someone to give him some attention," Shane said. "Go for it."

Caleb fell to his knees beside the large dog and wrapped his arms around Recon's neck. Recon didn't move, letting the young boy hug him tight.

"Cool," Carson said.

The boy's appreciation for his motorcycle made Shane smile fleetingly. "Do you know what a lug wrench is?"

Carson nodded.

"My tool kit is right over there." Shane nodded.

Carson dropped his shoes, jogged the short distance to the toolbox and then hurried back with the lug wrench.

"Good man," Shane said. "Thank you."

"Are they bothering you?" Rebecca appeared around the corner.

Shane glanced up from his work, glanced down, and then his eyes, almost beyond his control, went straight back to Rebecca. She was wearing a pretty sundress with a wide belt that emphasized her small waist and curvy hips. The dress was modest, and yet, Shane found it to be very sexy on Rebecca. As she drew closer, he could see that her cheeks were flushed, her pretty eyes were shining and her copper-brown curls framed her face in the most enchanting way. Today, Rebecca was happy.

"We're helping," Carson said.

"They're helping." Shane winked at Rebecca's eldest son.

Caleb was lying on his back in the grass, giggling and being licked on the face by Recon.

"Oh, my goodness." Rebecca's attention was captured by the vintage Indian. "Is this an original 841 or a replica?"

"It's no replica." Shane stood.

She circled the motorcycle, admiring his work.

"Did you restore this yourself?"

He nodded. "Most of the parts are original. I've been at it for years. I only use reproductions when I can't find the real deal."

"Your grandfather would have lost his mind over this, Carson," she said to her son. Then to him, she added, "My father was an Indian fanatic."

"What's so special about it?" Carson asked.

Shane was about to respond, but Rebecca put her arm around her son's shoulders and said, "This is *one* of only a thousand that were made specifically for the army during the Second World War. This could be in a museum, that's how special it is."

"Why'd they only make a thousand?" her son asked.

Rebecca gave a little shrug. "The Jeep came along and the Army didn't order any more."

Shane knew he was staring at her; he couldn't seem to help himself. He'd never known another woman to know the history of his prized motorcycle.

She looked at him, and he had to quickly avert his eyes before he renewed eye contact to cover up the fact that he had, in fact, been staring at her.

"Would you take a picture of my boys and me with it?"

Shane took her phone and took several pictures for

her. She scrolled through the pictures and then smiled at him.

"These are great. Thank you."

Standing so close to her, he could catch the fresh fruity scent of the shampoo she used in her hair. Rebecca Adams wasn't the prettiest woman he'd ever seen; she was, objectively, on the plain side. But there was something about her that attracted him. It was a magnetic pull that he didn't understand, and more important, he didn't necessarily like it.

Shane put some distance between them, taking the lug wrench back to his toolbox.

"Hi, Recon." Rebecca leaned down and scratched the dog around his ruff before she waved her hand to the boys.

"Come on, guys. I need you to change out of your clothes, grab some lunch and then call your dad. He misses you."

Carson and Caleb left the way they had come: chasing each other, screaming and laughing. Rebecca hesitated for a moment.

"Do you want to join us for lunch?"

Shane didn't want to look at her again, but he did out of politeness. "I appreciate the invite, but I had a pretty hardy lunch not too long ago."

"Well—" she walked backward a few steps "—if you change your mind…"

He nodded; he figured that they both knew he wasn't going to change his mind.

In spite of himself, he watched her walk away, liking the way she carried her shoulders and the soft sway of her hips.

Unexpectedly, Rebecca turned to face him again.

"Oh! I almost forgot to tell you. I met your sister-in-law today."

"Is that right? Which one?"

Rebecca laughed. "How many do you have?"

"Three."

"I met Savannah. At church."

"Let me guess." Shane walked back over to the motorcycle. "She put in a good word for me."

"As a matter of fact, she did."

"Well—" Shane knelt down by the back tire "—I don't just say this because she was talking about me. You can take what Savannah says to the bank. She doesn't know how to lie."

Rebecca quickly changed into jeans and a T-shirt and twisted her hair into a bun at the nape of her neck. The boys, now in their weekend clothes, met her in the kitchen.

"Did you hang everything up?"

"Yes," Carson said.

"No," Caleb said simultaneously.

Wordlessly, Rebecca pointed her finger toward the stairs leading to the second floor. Caleb took off running, which made her smile, even as she reminded him not to run in the house.

She made a quick lunch and then sent the boys back up to their room to start unloading the boxes that had been stacked neatly in the corner by the movers. While she washed the dishes, she looked out the window over the sink and watched Shane sitting in a lawn chair between his motorcycle and his front door, brushing Recon's coat. Much like the feeling she had about the German shepherd, Shane's outward appearance didn't seem to necessarily match his outward appearance. Savannah was an earnest soul—that was her impression of the woman—and her words only confirmed her own instinct about Shane Brand. There was a good man hidden beneath that beard, long hair and gruff personality. Thoughtfully, she wiped her hands on a dish towel, and by the time her hands were dry, she had made a decision. She had made one too many sandwiches, and instead of wrapping it up and putting it into the refrigerator, she wrapped it up in a paper towel and took it out to Shane.

"I know you said you weren't hungry." She held out the sandwich to him, spotting the open beer at his feet. "But I don't really consider *barley and hops* a hearty lunch."

Shane frowned at her for a split second before he silently took the sandwich. Recon took the opportunity, with his tail wagging, to greet her again. He licked her arm and she found a spot behind his ear that he liked to have scratched.

"I heard you playing the other night."

Shane had eaten half of the sandwich in one giant bite. He was chewing, so he couldn't answer right away. He swallowed hard, took a swig of beer and then said, "Ginny never minded me playing at night."

"Oh. I don't mind." She wanted to reassure him. "I…" Rebecca paused, not sure she wanted to share the fact that he had, unknowingly, given her a private concert. "Actually, I sat on the back porch stairs and listened to you."

Their eyes met, and she was so taken with the blue of his eyes. Those eyes drew her in and held her suspended for a minute before she could remind herself to look away.

"I've never heard anyone play a guitar like that before."

It had been sad and haunting and passionate. Shane played the guitar with all the emotion he couldn't seem to express in his expression or in his words. In so many ways, perhaps too many ways, Shane reminded her of her beloved father.

"Then I'll keep on playing for you."

She tucked her hands into her back pocket and shifted her weight onto one hip. "I wanted to talk to you about the new lease."

Shane crumpled the paper towel in his hand and she reached out to take it from him instinctively, as she would with Carson or Caleb.

"I like you, Shane. You seem like good people. You know the house, you take care of the yard and I could really use the extra income right now while I'm settling in and looking for work. So, if you want to stay on, I'll have the attorney send over the lease."

"I want to stay."

"Good. Then it's settled."

"Same rent?"

"Same rent."

He stood up, crossed the short distance to her and held out his hand. "I appreciate this, Rebecca."

"Of course, the old lease only accommodated for one pet. We'll have to change that to account for Top."

"I'll pay an additional pet deposit, if you'd like."

"No." She shook her head. "I'm just grateful that you saved her. Any news when she can come home?"

"Tomorrow."

"That soon?"

He nodded.

"That's wonderful, Shane. Caleb is going to be over the moon when he hears. I'm going to warn you now, he's going to beg you to see her."

"He can come see her."

"Well, if either of my boys start to wear out their welcome with you, don't be shy, just tell them the truth and they'll respect it."

He gave her another nod.

"Well, I'd better get back to work. Those boxes aren't going to unpack themselves."

The last time, she had something to add to the conversation—this time, it was Shane who stopped her from leaving.

"I forgot the thank you. For the lunch."

It wasn't his words that made her pulse quicken; it was the way he looked at her, like he really saw *her*. When Shane looked at her, it felt as if he was able to read all of the secrets of her soul. It was unnerving and, if she was being honest with herself, *exciting*.

"It was my pleasure, Shane."

Chapter Four

Rebecca was just breaking down the last box in the living room when an unexpected knock on the door made her jump. She dropped the box and walked over to the front door; she looked through the peephole and saw her sister, Kelly, standing on her front porch. They hadn't spoken to each other for weeks, and they hadn't seen each other in person since she moved to Bozeman. It was a fact of their strained relationship that just because they lived in the same town didn't mean that they would spend time together.

"Hi, Kell."

"I called. And sent a slew of texts."

Rebecca slipped her phone out of her back pocket and saw that there was a missed call and several text messages from Kelly. "I probably didn't hear it over the vacuum."

Kelly handed her a manila envelope. "Aunt Ginny's attorney accidentally sent this to me instead of you."

Rebecca took the envelope, which had been opened and then resealed with scotch tape. She stepped back, opening the door wider.

"Do you want to come in?"

Her sister hesitated, looking at the interior of the house, before she stepped across the threshold. Rebecca shut the door and opened the envelope while she followed her sister into the living room. Copies of Shane's new lease, with revised stipulations, were inside.

"Thank you for bringing these over." She set the envelope of the counter. "Do you want to sit down?"

Kelly was standing in the living room area, looking around with a disdainful look on her attractive face. Her sister, in her opinion, had managed to snag all of the good genes in the family. She was tall and slender; her hair was thick and wavy and shiny, while Rebecca was in a constant battle with frizz. Their mother, who hadn't been inclined to get her braces on her teeth, changed her mind with Kelly, and now her sister had perfect straight white teeth. And Kelly always had a sense of style; she always looked put together even if she was wearing jeans. It was the way Kelly wore the clothes, the way she carried herself, that set her apart from most women, especially her older sister.

"Talk about a time warp." Kelly didn't sit down. She held her designer bag, which was hooked on to her arm, next to her body as if she was afraid that something living in the purple shag carpet would grab it and take it back to the abyss.

"I know." Rebecca smiled. "When I was a kid, I

thought Aunt Ginny's purple shag carpet was the coolest thing I'd ever seen in my life."

"I never thought that." Kelly checked her phone.

There was a tense pause between them and then her sister turned toward her, and Rebecca, just by the pinched, superior look on Kelly's face, braced herself for a sisterly lecture.

"I assume that those leases mean that you are going to keep Shane as a tenant?"

It wasn't a secret that Kelly had been lobbying Aunt Ginny to find a new tenant, and once her sister knew that she was going to live in the house instead of sell, Kelly's desire to have Shane find a new place to live had transferred to her.

"What is your beef with Shane?" Rebecca crossed her arms in front of her body. "He was good to Aunt Ginny and, so far, he's been good to me and the boys."

"I don't have a beef with Shane," Kelly retorted. "I've known him for years. He's a nice guy."

"So? What's the problem?"

Kelly sighed in irritation. "You know I don't like to gossip."

Sure you do.

"But I know for a fact that Shane has brought drugs onto the premises."

The way her sister said the word *drugs*, with a dramatic flair, made it sound as if Shane was operating a drug ring out of the garage apartment. Kelly had, as far as she knew, never experimented with drugs and didn't drink. But Rebecca had experimented in her youth. And even though drugs weren't a part of her life anymore, she certainly didn't sit in judgment of those who did use them, for whatever reason.

"I've already handled that, Kell. As far as I'm concerned, he's welcome to stay as long as he follows the stipulations of the new lease. He's a veteran and that matters to me."

Kelly rolled her eyes in annoyance. "It's always about Dad with you."

They had both been close with their father, but Kelly was still bitter about his behavior after he came home from war. He could be mean at times, especially when he drank. And he would disappear for days sometimes, only to come back as if nothing had happened. Rebecca forgave her father years before he passed away, and she was glad now that she had.

"I've got to go." Her sister checked her phone again. She paused at the door. "I know you don't think this is true, Becca, but I worry about you and my nephews. You've already put them through so much with this ridiculous move. You wanted to fix Tim, and look where that got you. A divorce. Let's face it. You've always been attracted to broken people."

"Hi."

Shane was in the middle of a sneezing fit when Rebecca showed up at his door. Top had been home for a couple of weeks and one of her favorite places to sleep was curled up in the space between his shoulder and neck. He tried many different sleeping configurations— Recon and the kitten in the living room and him in the bed, or Recon with him in the bed—but nothing worked. Someone was unhappy unless they were all together. So Shane had given up and given in, and the kitten got to sleep where she wished. And he just dealt with the sneezing and swollen, itchy eyes. It wasn't the worst thing he'd ever dealt with in his life.

"Hi." He sneezed again.

"Bless you."

"Thank you."

"Kitten?"

He nodded as he blew his nose.

Rebecca showed him a pile of papers in her hand. "I have the new lease for you to review and sign."

He nodded. "Come on in. I'll look it over and sign it now."

Shane was proud of the fact that, in a short amount of time, he had turned his environment around. He didn't have a moment of hesitation inviting Rebecca into the garage apartment. It was clean and organized and, currently, full of balls and stuffed mice for a crazy kitten named Top. But the change wasn't just about Rebecca and the kitten. It was about Rebecca's boys. Carson and Caleb both wanted to regularly visit with Top and it was important to Shane that the boys had a clean place to spend time with the kitten they had a hand in saving. It was unexpected how quickly Rebecca and her sons had breathed new life into the old house. Ginny had been great, and he missed her, but she had left him alone to his own devices. She had rarely visited the courtyard and never entered his apartment. And he had appreciated the privacy and the quiet. Now he looked forward to hearing the sound of Carson's and Caleb's voices as they got off the school bus. Every weekday, he listened for them. And every weekday, they stopped by to see what he was doing before they headed inside. It was true—in a short period of time, they had changed his life. For the better.

Rebecca handed him the papers and immediately dropped to the ground on her knees to show Recon and the kitten some attention. Shane sat down on a bar stool at the small kitchen bar and began to read over the lease. It was standard—no real surprises. Out of the corner of his eye, he saw Top turn upside down in front of Rebecca, her black-and-pink paw pads up in the air, batting at a feather toy the landlady was holding.

"Top! You've already gotten so big!"

Shane hadn't expected it to happen so quickly, but he had fallen in love with that little rascal of a kitten. Yes, he had to load up on boxes of tissues and allergy medicine, but he didn't mind. Top was the funniest, sweetest little soul he'd ever encountered. And Recon and the kitten were best friends. In fact, Top had taken to riding on Recon's back like a jockey riding a horse. Every time Shane saw her do it, it made him laugh out loud.

Rebecca picked up the high-octane, wiggling kitten, kissed her on the head and then let her go. Top ran between Recon's legs, stood up on her hind legs, paws waving in the air, and "caught" Recon's tail. The dog didn't react.

"I can't believe how Recon treats her," she mused.

"Surprised me," Shane agreed. "It was love at first sight for those two."

"You're the reason they're still together," she said to him. "You saved her life."

"It was a group effort."

Rebecca stood up and wandered over to a bookshelf he had made in high school—it was a sturdy bookshelf that was carved from a fallen tree at Sugar Creek Ranch. It was one of the few things, other than his truck, motorcycle and his pets, that he cherished.

He was initialing the lease when Rebecca held up a picture frame. "Are these the men you served with?"

Shane didn't have to look at the picture; he knew which picture it was because it was the only one in the apartment. His fingers tightened on the pen until they ached, his heart began to race and he began to perspire, even though the AC was cranking. He closed his eyes for a brief moment, not wanting to draw attention to his reaction, swallowed hard and then said, "Yes. Those were my boys."

As if the dog sensed his discomfort, Recon moved to the spot by his feet and lay down. Top, who had run out of steam, sprawled out across Recon's back and promptly fell asleep. Shane signed and dated the lease and held it out for Rebecca to review.

"Do you have any questions? There were a couple of changes."

"It's all good."

Rebecca took the lease. "I'll make a copy of the signed lease for your records."

He walked her to the door and held it open for her.

Just outside the door, she paused. "'Bye, Recon. 'Bye, Top."

Almost on cue, he sneezed.

"If you're going to keep her, you're going to have to go to a doctor."

"Oh, I'm keeping her. She's family."

"Then I see an allergist in your future."

"I've got an appointment at the VA."

"That's smart," she said.

He nodded as he blew his nose, wishing that his eyes would stop itching.

"Well…" Rebecca smiled at him, her pretty eyes full

of acceptance as she looked at him. "I'll let you get on with your day."

He said goodbye but didn't really want her to leave. There was something about the kindness in this woman's smile that made him feel less anxious. There was sweetness in her eyes that made him want to look into them and never look away.

"How's it going in there?"

In the middle of the courtyard, Rebecca turned back to him. "With the unpacking?"

He nodded.

Her smile widened. "I'm finished!"

"Congrats on that."

"I know," she said, happily. "I know. I'm not sure what to do with myself for the rest of the day. Tomorrow, I start the search for work."

"What's your trade?"

Like a fisherman who had landed the catch of a lifetime, Shane had managed to get Rebecca to walk back toward him.

"I'm a hairstylist," she told him. "I want to open my own salon one day, but for now, I'll be happy being an independent contractor in someone else's salon."

"I have a friend who owns one of the salons in Bozeman," Shane said. "I can put in a good word for you."

"Seriously?"

He nodded.

Her face brightened and her cheeks turned a light shade of pink. "That would mean a lot, Shane."

"Is it okay if I give her your number?"

"Absolutely."

Shane sent Baily, his friend from high school, a text with Rebecca's information. In the text, he said that he would consider it a personal favor to him if Baily would meet with Rebecca.

"I can't promise anything."

Rebecca clasped her hands. "I know. I know. But it's my first lead."

They stood in silence for a moment, as they often did with each other, seeming as if there was always more to say, but neither of them knew *what* needed to be said.

"I want to pay you back," she finally said.

"No need."

"I could trim your beard and hair." Her eyes took stock of his disheveled appearance. "Free of charge. As a thank you."

Shane scratched his fingers through his beard. Rebecca wasn't the first person to comment on the fact that his beard was out of control. Savannah had mentioned it during his last performance, and Jessie, his younger sister, was always on him like a tick on a dog about personal grooming.

"I don't want it gone," he cautioned her.

"Just a trim." When she smiled at him, it melted his heart a centimeter more. "I promise."

He kept on scratching his beard; he was used to it, scruffy as it was. He might feel a bit naked without it.

"When you get settled in a salon, I'll think about coming to see you. How's that?"

"Oh, we don't have to wait," she said. "I have a chair in the house."

Somehow, Shane found himself walking beside Rebecca to the main house. He hadn't intended to have his beard and hair trimmed today—or any other day in the near future—and yet, here he was, tagging along with Rebecca just to extend the time they were spending together. He just liked to be around her. She was kind and had good energy.

He followed her into the house, noting that she had kept Ginny's furnishings in place. But the house had a clean, lemony smell to it, and there were small pots of flowers in the kitchen. The house reflected Rebecca's upbeat personality.

"It looks good in here."

"Thanks. It was a chore. Can I get you something to drink? Water?"

He shook his head.

What are you doing, Shane?

This was the time to change his mind; this was the time to politely thank Rebecca for the offer and get the heck out of Dodge.

Rebecca smiled and waved her hand for him to follow. He hesitated, and then he shrugged his shoulders and headed down a narrow hallway with wooden planked floors that creaked when he stepped on them. He'd never been to this part of the house.

"Have a seat." Rebecca seemed way too excited about the prospect of taking scissors to his hair. She walked with a bounce in her step, which made her thick, curly ponytail sway back and forth like a pendulum. He suddenly understood Top's desire to reach out and bat something with her paw. Shane felt like reaching out and batting that bouncing ponytail. At the end of the hall, Rebecca went into a bathroom, which she had turned into a mini-salon, with a chair and all of her supplies on the sink counter.

"It's been too long since I've had my hands in a head of hair." She retrieved a smock out of the linen closet. "I think this one will fit you."

Shane stared at the smock but didn't move to take it or to take a seat.

"Come on, Shane." She laughed. "I promise I won't bite."

Every time he thought that he was going to turn and leave, his body did the opposite. He let Rebecca help him into the smock, which was ridiculous, and then he sat down.

"Ready?"

"Not really."

Rebecca lowered the back of the chair until his head was over the sink. She had already turned on the water to get it hot.

"Let me know if it's too warm, okay?"

He nodded and kept his fingers threaded together on his chest. He had no idea that he had gotten so attached to his beard and hair that the thought of cutting them made him anxious. He was an army man; he needed to suck it up and get the stupid trim.

"Just close your eyes, Shane. Relax and enjoy it. The customers at my old salon voted me best scalp massage two years in a row."

Shane breathed in and let out his breath, slow and steady. And then he closed his eyes and let her take control. First she wrapped his face and neck in a hot towel, and then she poured cupfuls of warm water onto his hair. The smell of the shampoo, citrusy, was the same scent that Shane had caught on Rebecca's hair. It reminded him of her and he liked it. Her strong fingers began to massage his scalp. How long had it been since he allowed any woman to touch him? The longer she massaged, the more relaxed he became. The last thing he remembered was focusing in on Rebecca's soft inhalation and exhalation of breath as she worked.

"Shane?"

He could hear someone in the distance calling out his name.

"Shane?"

Shane's eyes popped open and he jumped out of the chair, yanking the towels off his face. He spun around, his hands up in front of him in a defensive position, forcing his brain to reengage and assess his surroundings.

"You fell asleep," Rebecca said in a calm voice. "I didn't mean to startle you."

Inside his body, the adrenaline was making his hands shake, but on the outside, he repositioned his mask and tried to smile at her.

"That must've been one hell of a massage you gave me."

Her body, which she had been holding tensely, relaxed and she patted the chair. "I told you. Best scalp massage two years in a row."

Chapter Five

"Hey! What are you doing out here before noon?" Rebecca waved at Shane.

He turned toward the sound of her voice and waited for her to catch up with him.

"Grass needs cutting."

Lately she had noticed that Shane was appearing earlier and earlier and without a beer glued to his hand. He still drank—his recycling bins were evidence of that—but he didn't drink in the courtyard during the day, and she noticed that he didn't drink in front of Caleb and Carson. Both of her boys, but especially Carson, liked spending time with Shane. And even though she was cautious with anyone new spending time with her boys, she didn't mind them hanging out with Shane, particularly when she could keep an eye on everyone from the kitchen window.

She smiled up at Shane when she reached him, still surprised by how handsome this man was now that his beard was trimmed and his thick brown hair had been cut to collar length. Shane had a strong square jawline and chin; he hadn't been covering up a flaw in his facial structure with that beard. But Rebecca had the feeling that he had been *hiding* behind that beard. Even when he looked at her with his bright aqua-blue eyes, she felt as if he was working to hide himself from the world. Of course, now that he had Top, his eyes were red, not from a hangover necessarily, but from allergies. Today, his eyes were puffy and she knew that meant the kitten had insisted on sleeping on his pillow.

She looked around at the yard. "Huh. It does. And, I see plenty of weeds I could pull."

"I'll get to them."

"I'll help. I don't mind. Gets me outside on this beautiful day," she said. "Guess what?"

"What?"

"I met with your friend Baily and I'm starting there on Monday. I'm going to start bringing all of my supplies to the salon tomorrow. I already scoped out my station, and so far, everyone seems super nice."

"Good news."

"*Great* news." She couldn't stop smiling. "I'll be handling all the walk-ins until I build my clientele, and Baily says there's a lot of foot traffic because we are so close to the university."

While she was talking, Shane was pulling the lawn mower out of the shed.

"Did you put in a good word for me?"

Shane checked the gas in the lawn mower before he straightened upright and looked at her. In a rare moment of levity, he took off his baseball cap, shook his hair like he was in a shampoo commercial and said, "Look what you did for me, and you didn't have all that much to work with."

She laughed and reached out to squeeze his forearm. "I had plenty to work with. Okay. Let me change into my weed-pulling clothes."

As she always did, she remembered she had one more thing to say to Shane, so she turned around and headed back to him.

"I almost forgot! Savannah called and said that you have a gig tomorrow night."

He nodded.

"Well. Why didn't you tell me?"

"Didn't think about it, I suppose."

"Well, Savannah invited me, and I'm going to go. I want to hear you sing."

Shane played guitar in the courtyard almost every night, but he never sang. When Savannah had told her last Sunday that her brother-in-law had an amazing voice and wrote incredible lyrics, Rebecca wanted to hear for herself. It had been too long since she had a girl's night out. She deserved one.

"Who's going to watch the boys?"

"Your sister, Jessie," Rebecca said. "I trust Savannah and Savannah trusts Jessie with Amanda, so…"

"I'd better get to it." Shane gestured to the tall grass.

She wasn't sure how to read his expression—he didn't seem all that pleased that she was going to come see him perform. She almost asked him, but decided just to let it go. Sometimes she felt as if she had known Shane for years; other times, he seemed like a total stranger. In truth, and she would never admit this to

Kelly, Shane Brand did remind her of her father. Pull her close and then push her away.

They spent the rest of the afternoon working on grooming the lawn. She liked to pull weeds—it gave her a sense of accomplishment to see the pile of weeds growing taller and taller as she worked her way down the row of shrubs. Shane had his earbuds in his ears and he was focused on getting the grass cut, only stopping to refill the tank with gasoline. Shane had just finished mowing and was getting the edger out of the shed when Rebecca heard the bus pull up to the house. As she always did, she smiled at the thought of seeing her sons come home. Caleb had settled into his new life—he was easygoing and really liked his third-grade teacher, Mrs. Pedraza. Caleb had already made friends, which was his way. His father had sent him a new camera as an early birthday gift, and Caleb was obsessed with taking pictures when he was finished with his homework. Carson, on the other hand, who had always been a square peg in a round hole, hadn't settled in as well. She worried about him. The closest person he had as a friend right now was Shane.

"The boys are home," she called out to Shane. "Why don't we take a break? I have lemonade."

Shane nodded, sneezed and pulled a bandanna out of his pocket to wipe the sweat from his neck and brow. Caleb came running around the corner, dragging his backpack on the ground.

"Hi, Mom!" Her youngest barreled into her and gave her a hug. She kissed him on the top of the head and hugged him tight before he wiggled away.

"Hi, Shane!"

"How was school?" she asked.

"Good." Caleb dropped his backpack and ran over to Shane.

"Where's your brother?" Rebecca knelt back down to pull a few more weeds.

"He's coming," Caleb called over his shoulder. To Shane, he asked, "Can I go see Top?"

"Let's get Recon and Top. They probably need a break."

Rebecca watched as Caleb walked beside Shane, noticing that he had gone through another growth spurt. He was all legs and lankiness, like his father.

"Hey." Carson came into sight.

"Hi." She gave him a hug. Now that he was in fifth grade, he didn't tolerate hugs for quite as long as she wanted to give them.

"How was your day?" she asked, hoping that it was going to be a positive report. The one major reason she had hesitated to move was because of Carson. It had taken him years to build his core group of friends; to take him away from them hadn't been an easy decision. But after her father died and after her marriage failed, it seemed like fate that Aunt Ginny had left her this house.

Carson shrugged.

"It'll get better. I promise." Even as she said the words, she wasn't so sure that it was true.

"Well, I have good news. I got a job today," she told him as she brushed his longish bangs out of his eyes. "It looks like you could use a trim yourself."

"I'm okay."

Shane, Caleb, Recon and Top emerged from the garage apartment and she saw the light return to Carson's face. He loved Recon and Top, and when he got to spend time with Shane, working on the motorcycle, those were the times he seemed most happy in Montana.

Carson piled his backpack on top of Caleb's and sat down in the grass near where the kitten was pouncing on an imagined foe.

"Will she be okay out here?" Rebecca asked, concerned.

"If I bring Recon out here and leave her in, she cries the whole time. If she's out here with Recon, she only goes as far as he goes."

She put her hands on her hips and shook her head. "They are an odd couple."

Rebecca and Caleb went into the house to get the pitcher of lemonade and some cups. When they returned, Carson and Shane seemed to be engrossed in an important conversation.

"Mom."

"Yes?" She poured Shane a glass of lemonade first.

"Did you know that Shane played baseball?"

Rebecca handed the glass of lemonade to the army veteran. "No. I didn't."

"I played a little in high school." Shane took the cup with a thank you.

"*And* in college. He was a *pitcher.*" Carson was slightly out of breath with excitement as he talked. "*And* he said that he would help me with *my* pitching."

"You played in college?" She sat down in the grass, cross-legged, once she had served everyone, including herself, a glass of lemonade.

"He had a scholarship," Carson interjected.

"You must have been very good," Rebecca said, watching Caleb with the kitten and Recon from the corner of her eye.

"I'd say I was."

The one thing she'd figured out about Shane was the fact that he wasn't big on bragging about himself. He was humble in that way.

"Did you want to play pro ball?" She took a sip of the tart lemonade.

"All my life." It was a rare admission, a rare peek into Shane's past.

"What happened to that dream?"

Shane's broad shoulder's stiffened beneath his sweat-stained T-shirt. There was a far-off look in his eyes that was fleeting, but Rebecca saw it.

He cleared his throat and looked away from her. "Just life. No different than anybody else, I reckon."

Shane, Rebecca was discovering, was the king of noncommittal responses.

"I wasn't cut out for college," Rebecca said, instead of pushing him for an answer. "I always loved makeup and doing my friends' hair. Trade school made sense for me."

"But can he help me with my pitching, Mom, so I can make a team during the summer?" Carson, who had been waiting patiently for his turn in the conversation piped up during a lull between the adults.

"We'll see," she said. "Caleb? You and your brother go on inside the house and start your homework. I'll be in in a minute."

The boys reluctantly left the courtyard, scooping up their backpacks off the ground and walking at a snail's pace to the back door of the house.

"You've got two really good boys, Rebecca."

"I agree." She smiled proudly as she stood up and

brushed the grass off her jeans. "Well, I'd better go in and start dinner."

Shane helped her gather up the cups and pitcher of lemonade. And then, in a rare moment of openness, he said, "I loved playing ball. I was good at it. Damn good at it, actually. But only a few ever make it to the pros."

Rebecca moved out of the path of the sun so she could see his face.

"I went to college to be an architect."

"Couldn't you still be an architect? Architect by day, rock star by night?"

"No. It didn't work out that way for me."

"But why not?" Rebecca was of the mind that anything was possible, in some shape or form, if a person put their mind to it.

"In the end, I didn't get a degree in architecture." This time, Shane didn't avert his eyes. He let her see a glimpse into his soul, for only a split second. "I got a degree in war."

"Hello, stranger."

Shane was loading his guitar into the truck when he noticed Savannah walking toward him. He shut the passenger door to his truck and greeted his sister-in-law with a warm hug. He liked Savannah; unlike many people in his family, she didn't push him to join them for the traditional family Sunday brunch at Sugar Creek. Unlike most of his family, she didn't act like she wanted him to transform into the Shane before Afghanistan. That Shane was dead.

"Wow! Shane! You look so handsome. I can actually see your face." Savannah was as bubbly and up-beat as always.

"Jessie's inside with Rebecca, if you're looking for her."

"I saw her car." Savannah pointed to the Range Rover in the driveway. "But I was actually looking for you. It seemed weird to come here without at least stopping by to say hello."

"I was just getting ready to head out." He leaned back against his truck. "Are you coming?"

"Of course." Savannah gave one definitive nod. "I don't miss your shows if I can help it."

"Who else from the fam is coming?"

Savannah held up a finger for each family member she named. "Bruce, Liam, Kate, me. Gabe's in town, so he'll be there. Jessie's babysitting for Rebecca. Your parents are babysitting for me. So, five. Six including Rebecca."

"Then I'll see you all there. I've got to go get set up." Shane pushed away from the truck and gave his sister-in-law another hug.

"I can't wait for Rebecca to hear you sing." His sister-in-law's green eyes were sparkling with excitement for the evening out ahead. "Don't you just love Rebecca? I tell you, she's the sweetest person I've ever met."

With Savannah, he often found it difficult to fudge the truth; she was such an honest, earnest person. So he was honest with her when he said, "The more time I spend with her, the more time I want to spend with her."

Rebecca had a mixture of emotions as she left her boys in the care of Jessie. Jessie was young and playful and had the same blue eyes as Shane. But she could tell that Shane's little sister could be a firm hand if the fun became too rowdy, which was a real possibility with two boys.

"I can't remember the last time I had a girls' night out," she said from the passenger seat of Savannah's Cadillac SUV.

"There will be some men there, too," Savannah elaborated. "You're actually going to meet three of Shane's brothers and one additional sister-in-law. And you met Jessie today. Basically, you are being inundated by the Brands today."

"How many more are there?" she asked, only half in jest.

"We are a group." Savannah laughed. "But not too many more, and you'll know every Brand in the greater Bozeman area."

They talked nonstop all the way to Club XI. Ever since the day they met, they had always ended a conversation only because they had to go—not for the lack of anything to say. They texted several times a day and talked on the phone at least once per day. They followed each other's lives on social media. And, of course, they sat with each other every Sunday at church. Meeting Savannah had gone a long way to making Bozeman feel more like home for Rebecca.

As they pulled into a parking space, Rebecca flipped down the shade to check her lipstick in the mirror. She had taken extra time to tame the brown mass of curls that was her hair; she'd put on mascara *and* lipstick. And she'd dug one of her favorite dresses out from the back of her closet; this dress cinched her in at the waist, emphasizing her hourglass figure. When she looked in the mirror, Rebecca had twirled around and felt genuinely proud of the way she had put herself together for her first night out in Bozeman.

"You look beautiful." Savannah unbuckled her seat belt.

"I was thinking the same thing about you."

As they walked into the bar, Rebecca was wondering if Shane would notice her transformation from supermom to woman-on-the-town.

"There's Bruce." Savannah pointed to a long table near the stage.

They wound their way through the crowd. Rebecca had heard that Shane drew a crowd, but it was standing room only. It was the first time she had gone to a bar where she felt like a middle-aged person, even though she wouldn't categorize herself as middle-aged just yet. Most of the people in the crowd were college-aged and she noticed that there was a large number of nubile, young, fresh-faced girls gathered near the stage. Shane's music obviously appealed to a younger, more female audience.

For the next hour, Rebecca was introduced to some of Shane's older brothers. She met Bruce, a died-in-the-wool cowboy, straight out of a Western movie; Liam, a tall, handsome, country large-animal vet, and his lovely horse-training wife, Kate. She also met Gabe, who in her mind had the closest resemblance to Shane, minus the beard. Gabe was also a horse trainer and long-distance hauler for high-end equines. To Rebecca, who had lived a fairly routine, quiet American life, the over-achieving Brands seemed so glamorous and beautiful. Sitting with them made her feel a bit dumpy and out of place. But Savannah, who was so pretty with her long auburn hair, fair skin and freckles, and emerald green eyes, always made her feel at ease.

"I'm glad you came."

Rebecca heard Shane's voice from behind her; it felt as if she would be able to pick up on that deep, gravelly voice from even the loudest of rooms. She turned in her chair, and for some reason, her heart started to beat faster. This was just Shane—the man who cut her lawn and saw her sweating in her yard clothes. This was just Shane—the man who had become a friend to her and her boys. And yet, seeing him outside of their private courtyard world for the first time felt special, if only to her.

Shane greeted his family next and then he took the stage. With his acoustic guitar, he stood alone on the stage in front of the microphone. Just his presence on stage made the room quiet. When he said hello to the crowd, there was an explosion of clapping, hooting and whistling.

Savannah reached over and squeezed her hand in excitement. "You are going to *love* this."

Then Shane began singing his first song. It was an original, and the moment he began to sing, a hush fell over the crowd. On the first note, before Shane had sung one whole word, the hairs stood up on Rebecca's arm. Everything Shane couldn't say in person, all of the words he couldn't seem to dislodge from his mouth, all of the emotions he kept bottled-up inside, he poured into his lyrics. Rebecca felt everything—his pain, his anger, his sorrow and his love and his joy. Everyone in the room, including her, couldn't take their eyes off Shane. His rough, lived-in voice, and the music that he composed for the lyrics that he wrote, captivated her.

The man may have wanted to be a baseball player or an architect, but what he had become was a gifted musician, lyricist and singer. Shane Brand was a star.

Shane took a break, but Rebecca didn't bother to try to get a moment with him. He was swamped by fawning college girls offering him beers and, no doubt, phone numbers. Shane took the beers, but Rebecca doubted he would take phone numbers. In the time she had lived in Montana, she hadn't seen Shane with a woman. He was a loner and the consummate bachelor. Of course, she didn't spend every waking hour with him. When he left the property, he could be seeing women. And it wasn't really her business either way.

When Shane retook the stage, she could see by the glassy look in his eyes that the beers he'd been drinking were taking hold. He lit a cigarette, took a couple of drags and then tucked the burning cigarette under a string. During the first part of the set, Shane hadn't focused on her; but that wasn't true during the second part of the set. With the stage still surrounded by college girls vying for his attention, Shane looked past them and straight at her while he sang. To have someone, at least from her point of view, sing to her, single her out as important, made her feel special in a way she had never experienced before in her life. She had had two serious relationships and had married once, and never felt in those relationships the way she felt in this one moment with her friend Shane.

"I'd like to finish tonight with a song I just wrote. I've never played it before, so ya'll are gonna be the first to hear it."

All eyes were on Shane as he continued in a raspy, loose voice.

"I wrote this about someone I met recently. Someone who managed to change my life for the better without even trying—the song is 'Pretty Eyes.'"

Chapter Six

Rebecca was on her feet with the rest of the crowd, clapping for Shane as he finished his final song. The song—that beautiful, soulful song—had brought her to tears. The minute he started to sing, tears began to stream down her face, and as fast as she could wipe them away, more appeared. There were too many clues he had left for her that were unmistakably between them. Simple moments that hadn't seemed meaningful to her had obviously held some significance for Shane. Shane was thanking her with this song, she was sure of it. But she had no idea what he was thanking her for.

"That song was about you." Savannah was wiping tears off her own cheeks. "Wasn't it?"

"I can't be sure," she said in a voice only loud enough for her friend to hear. "But I think so."

"I know it is," her friend said. "He was looking right at you."

Shane, with his guitar slung on his back, made it through the crowd to his family's table. He'd had one too many beers, Rebecca noticed, because he was wobbly on his feet. She blended into the background while his family poured love and praise on Shane. She had always known that he was a man with a wounded soul; she had no idea, until tonight, how much emotional pain Shane carried with him on a daily basis. Her sister's words echoed in her brain about all of her decisions being about the helplessness she felt, as a child, when their father couldn't shake Vietnam. There was something in her, like a flower opening its petals for the sun, which had opened to Shane while he sang. Was she only attracted to men who needed fixing? Did that mean that her friendship, her growing fondness and her budding feelings for Shane all link back to her daddy issues?

"Rebecca."

He had never said her name quite like he did tonight, like satin sheets on bare skin. There was a suggestion that made her tingle in almost forgotten places when he said her name. He didn't try to hug her or touch her, but the beers had made him looser, more uninhibited, than she had ever seen him.

Before she could tell him how much she had enjoyed his performance, he swayed in her direction and said, "I'd like to drive you home."

Savannah quickly chimed in. "Whoa. Slow down there, cowboy. You're not driving anybody anywhere. Rebecca came with me and I'll drive you both home."

"Sugar Creek's in the other direction," Shane said with slightly slurred words.

"No matter," Savannah said, putting her arm around her husband Bruce's waist.

"Is it far out of the way?" Rebecca asked her friend.

"No," her friend responded.

"Sure it is," Shane countered. "By about an hour round trip."

Savannah said to Rebecca. "He can't drive like this."

The night, which had elated her, was being drained of the magic now that the reality of Shane's tendency to overindulge was front and center. She knew Shane drank at night. She knew he, at times, drank heavily at night. But until now, she'd never seen him drunk.

"I've only had one glass of wine tonight. I'll drive him home. That way, you can get home to Amanda and I won't have to drive Shane back here tomorrow to get his truck."

Savannah looked up at her husband.

"You don't mind?" Bruce asked her.

"No. Not at all."

"But can she drive a stick shift?" Shane asked the circle of family members that had gathered.

Rebecca slanted him a *look* that she mostly reserved for her sons when they were disobedient. "Yes, she *can* and yes, she *does*."

She saw respect on the faces of his brothers' and sisters-in-law's faces. Shane could be intimidating and kept people at a distance with his anger and bad attitude. That wasn't the kind of friendship they had developed.

She held out her hand. "Keys."

Rebecca had to admit that Shane's antique truck was trickier to drive than she had imagined. Her bravado in the bar faded slightly when she pulled out onto the road. The steering was stiff and the gears were stiff and the brakes were not as responsive as she was used to in modern vehicles. It took all of her concentration to navigate at night on still-unfamiliar roads. Luckily, Shane had fallen asleep, or passed out, in the passenger seat, so she didn't have to contend with him while she was focused on her driving.

Suddenly Shane's head bobbed forward. "Did you like your song?"

"Yes." *Like* was an understatement. "I did."

"You have pretty eyes," he muttered and then seemed to fall back asleep.

She had never thought of her eyes as pretty before; she hadn't thought that much about her was pretty. She had been the cute, quirky girl who had developed too young. She'd been teased about her breasts and her "birthing" hips and her "thunder" thighs in middle school, and the teasing didn't stop until she graduated from high school. Perhaps that's why she had settled on the men she had—no self-esteem. But now she liked what she saw in the mirror. Was she Angelina Jolie? No. But she was Rebecca Adams, and that was good enough for her.

She silently thanked God when she pulled the truck into their driveway. She'd started to get the hang of it along the way, yet it still felt foreign and odd to drive.

"Shane." She touched his arm lightly. "We're home."

He slowly opened his eyes and looked at her. "Hi."

"Hi." She smiled at him fondly because she couldn't help herself. "We're home."

"Let me get your door for you." He fumbled with the passenger door handle.

"I can get my own door, Shane. I'm right here."

"No," he insisted. "My mom worked damn hard to

make me a gentleman and I want you to enjoy it. Just sit right there and let me get your door."

Shane got out of the truck, slammed the door too hard, walked around the front of the truck, using the hood as a way to steady his walking, and then opened the driver's-side door for her.

He held out his hand to help her out, even though the ground, because Shane had lowered the truck's frame, was only a foot away.

"Thank you," she said, slipping her purse over her shoulder.

Shane shut the door and took the keys she had offered him, but didn't let go of her hand. Instead, he held on to it, slipped his hand beneath her hair to her neck, bent down and kissed her on the lips. It was a quick kiss, but it was enough of a kiss that she could feel the warmth of his skin and softness of his beard on his face.

Caught off guard and unnerved, Rebecca didn't say anything or move as Shane let his hands fall away from her. He stared at her and she stared back, and then, wordlessly, he turned and walked toward his apartment. She heard Recon barking and the sound of the apartment door shutting, and that's when she finally turned toward her own home. Rebecca reached up and touched her lips, which still felt tingly from Shane's kiss. A kiss from Shane hadn't been a part of the evening's plan for her. Had it been a part of his plan? Or was the kiss only a side effect of the beer? As she opened the door to her house, Rebecca couldn't honestly say which scenario she wanted to be true. Yes, there was no doubt she was attracted to Shane, as a man, as a veteran, as a talented singer and songwriter, and as a friend. And, yes, she wanted to be in a long-term relationship one day with a man who loved her and loved her sons as his own. She wanted to grow old with someone; she even wanted to give marriage another try. But could a man with so many demons mingled in with so much good be the kind of man who could promise forever and mean it? It seemed like an awfully long shot, one that a single mother with two boys to provide for should be extremely cautious to take.

Rebecca didn't see Shane for a couple of days, which turned out to be the right path for her. She was busy setting up her station at the salon and coordinating her work schedule with her boys' schedule. Baily understood the plight of single mothers and was very flexible with the hours her contractors could work. Rebecca could schedule clients as early or as late as she needed because Baily had given her a key to the salon and the code for the alarm. But even though she hadn't seen Shane, he was often on her mind. She could still feel his lips on hers; she would tear up, even when she was in public, when the lyrics to the song he wrote for her came into her mind. Her feelings for Shane were jumbled and confusing and she felt *shy* about seeing her friend even though she had never felt shy around him before. All she had ever felt with Shane was a kinship and a comfort.

"Mom!"

She was in her makeshift salon in the house packing some final supplies when Carson called for her.

"I'm back here."

Carson, his cheeks red from running, and the light brown hair on his forehead darkened with perspiration, appeared in the doorway. He had his baseball glove on his right hand and a baseball his father had sent to him in the mail in his left.

"Shane wants to take me to a baseball field to practice pitching. Can I go?"

Rebecca paused from her chore and looked at her son's expectant, excited face. Carson was still having difficulty fitting in at school and he gravitated to Shane for companionship. She didn't mind his growing bond with Shane—Shane was a good man, regardless of his issues—but she still wanted Carson to develop friendships with peers. Joining a summer league might be the answer for Carson. But she didn't let people just take off with her sons, not even someone she had known for a while like Shane.

"Please."

Carson had kept up with his grades even with the upheaval of the move and he did his chores with the rare reminder. If going to a baseball field with Shane felt like a reward to her son, then she needed to finish packing later.

"Okay. I'll take you."

"You don't have to," Carson was quick to say. "Shane can drive me."

Rebecca knew that Carson wanted to ride in the red truck with the flames painted on the side in the worst way, but her driving was a nonnegotiable.

"I'll drive," she reiterated. "Do me a favor. Go get Caleb and meet me at the car and tell Shane we'll follow him over."

Rebecca locked the front door and then walked, keys in hand, toward her Camry. Carson and Caleb were at the car, per her request, but Shane was also standing by the trunk of her car, holding a netted bag full of what looked to be baseball equipment.

"Hi, Rebecca." Shane seemed happy to see her.

And she was, in fact, happy to see him. It had only been a few days, and even with her confused feelings, she had missed his company. She had missed her friend.

"Hi, Shane."

"Mind if I hitch a ride with you? No sense taking two vehicles."

"All right."

She popped the trunk so Shane could put his equipment in the car and then waited for him to get into the passenger side. Rebecca could see Carson's face in the rearview mirror and the spark she saw in his eyes was heartening.

"Everyone buckled in?" she asked as she cranked the engine.

Caleb yelled, "Yes!"

"That was my eardrum," Rebecca said. "Did you really need to scream like that, Caleb?"

Her youngest son laughed as if he had told the best joke and then whispered, "Yes."

Rebecca sneaked a quick glance at Shane's profile. He wasn't acting at all like a man who remembered that he had kissed her. He was acting like the same old, good ol' friendly Shane. And she was grateful for that, because it helped set her at ease around him. This Shane she knew how to handle. Romantic, let-me-kiss-you Shane, not so much.

At the road entrance, she asked Shane. "Where are we going?"

"We're going to my old high school. It's the best field

around. Take a left here and go straight. I'll help you navigate along the way."

Perhaps to someone who didn't know Shane, a trip to his old high school would seem a common event. But Rebecca knew differently. Savannah had, in passing, told Rebecca about all the scouts that would come to see Shane play ball. He had been the fastest high school pitcher in the state of Montana and he could also smack the ball out of the park. Everyone in Bozeman thought that Shane would go pro. That all changed when he enlisted after his friend died in Iraq. Shane, according to Savannah, gave up his scholarships and his pro-ball dreams and enlisted in the army. So Shane returning to his high school was like him returning to a scene of a crime. The memories of a life he had lived, which was a sharp contrast from the promise of his youth to the reality of his adulthood, might be horrible for Shane. The fact that he wanted to help Carson with his pitching on a field that he knew was the best in town made her feel closer to him as a person and a friend.

She pulled into a parking space at the high school. There was a group of cheerleaders practicing in the distance and some kids milling about after school, but the baseball field was empty. Rebecca met Shane by the trunk.

"Thank you for this, Shane."

He pulled the bag of equipment out of the trunk and slung it over his shoulder. "I want him to make that team."

"Me, too."

Carson was staring, wide-eyed at the field. "I've never thrown that far from the pitcher's mound, Shane."

Shane put his hand on Carson's shoulder. "If you

can put a controlled ball in my glove from that mound, you will be the most sought-after pitcher in the summer leagues. Do you trust me?"

Rebecca watched her son's face, the look in his light brown eyes, when he said with a nod. "I trust you, Shane."

"Good." The veteran kept his hand on Carson's shoulder while he marched them forward. "Then let's get to work."

Shane stepped onto the field that used to be his home, and memories, so many memories, barreled over him like a tidal wave. These memories were so strong, almost tangible in their strength, that for a split second, Shane felt weak in the knees. This was where he had shined as a high school student. He was the pitcher; his best friend, Dustin, was his catcher. Together, they were an unbeatable team, taking their team to the state championship. An image appeared of the last time he'd seen Dustin, proudly wearing his marine uniform, a goofy grin on his face and a shaved head from his recent stint in boot camp. They had both earned full-ride scholarships to different universities; they both felt the call of their country to Dustin's older brother, Jeff, was killed in Iraq. Dustin signed up with the marines and Shane signed up with the army. Two of them went to war, but only one of them came back alive. There wasn't a day that went by that Shane didn't miss his best friend.

"People say I can't pitch because I'm a south paw." Carson was standing on the pitcher's mound, his shoulders slumped forward in defeat before he even got started.

"I don't know who these people are, but don't listen

to them. They don't know what they're talking about. I can name plenty of famous left-handed pitchers."

Carson, of course, challenged him to do it. This was a challenge he was up for.

"Lefty Grove, Warren Spahn, Randy Johnson, Sandy Koufax, Whitey Ford, Tom Glavine." Shane looked at his companion to see if he was sufficiently impressed. *"Babe Ruth."*

"Babe Ruth?"

"He could hit *and* pitch." Shane held up his left hand and flexed his fingers. "Let me see. Anyone else I can name? Oh, yeah. Shane Brand."

Carson started to smile, which was the whole point for Shane. He had his mother's smile. "And soon-to-be-famous Carson Adams."

For the next hour, Shane worked with Carson on his stance, on how he threw the ball, on precision and force. Everything the kid would need to know to put the ball where he wanted it over the plate.

"Can you teach me how to throw a curveball?"

"You must walk before you run, Grasshopper."

Carson's eyebrows lifted. "Grasshopper?"

"Okay—*Kung Fu* may be too old a reference for you." Shane laughed. "I'll teach you when you're ready. How's that? First I want to see you get it over this plate and into my glove."

Rebecca had been watching them intently from the bleachers. He didn't mind that her eyes were on him; in fact, he liked it. And he liked a day like today—spending time with the boys and their mother, doing something that he used to love and was, at one time, pretty darn good at doing.

Shane squatted behind the plate, pulled down the face shield on the catcher's mask and held out his glove.

"Put it right here, Carson. Just like I taught you."

Carson wound up for the pitch and then threw the ball. The ball landed short of the plate and bounced into his glove.

"Good try!" Rebecca shouted from the bleachers.

Carson looked disappointed.

Shane threw the ball back to him. "Don't give up. Try again. You can do it."

It took Carson five more tries, but his last pitch landed smack dab in the center of Shane's glove. Carson, with a surprised look on his face, jumped up and down and performed a celebration dance on the mound.

"That's it!" Shane tossed the ball back to him. "You thought about where you wanted to put it and your arm followed."

Shane took off his catcher's mask and mitt and grabbed a bat.

"This is your pop quiz, Carson." He did something he hadn't done since college—he stepped up to the plate. "Throw me something that I can knock out of the park."

For the second time that day, Carson put the ball right over the plate. Shane swung the bat, and he heard that wonderful "crack" as the bat hit the ball. Shane pointed to the bleachers on the other side of the field, tossed the bat behind him and began to run the bases.

"And the crowd went wild!" Shane raised his arms in the air as he ran from first to second base.

Carson chased after him, and next thing Shane knew, Caleb had caught them at third base and the three of them were racing for home. The boys' laughter and happy, red-cheeked faces felt like a salve on a wound that had been scraped open the minute he walked onto this field. Fighting to catch his breath, Shane half slid, half fell onto home plate, and then Carson and Caleb piled on top of him.

"Don't smash him." Rebecca was walking toward them with Caleb's camera in her hand.

Still laughing, the boys rolled off him, into the red clay, and he sat up, coughing and struggling to get some air in his lungs.

Carson stood up, brushed off his pants and offered his ungloved hand to Shane. Still coughing, his chest noticeably rising and falling from the running, he accepted his young friend's hand.

"Thanks, buddy," Shane said, his pitiful state of fitness being hammered home. He'd only run the bases and he was gasping for air and coughing like a ninety-year-old smoker.

Carson looked up at him with a very serious, very grown-up expression and said, "You really need to quit smoking."

With a winded laugh, Shane put his arm around Carson's shoulders. Carson had seen an open pack of cigarettes on his kitchen counter. "I quit right now."

"Promise?" his young protégée asked.

"Promise."

"Don't make a promise to him you aren't willing to keep, Shane," Rebecca cautioned.

"I'm a man of my word." He looked directly into Rebecca's eyes so she could see how serious he was. "I keep my promises."

Chapter Seven

After the baseball field, they stopped off at a restaurant and shared a meal. Then Rebecca was convinced by the three males in the vehicle to stop for ice cream. Shane couldn't pinpoint a better day in his recent history. He had always wanted a family of his own—he figured he would have had at least a couple of kids by his age. But for years, he wasn't able to let a woman close to him. There were plenty of women in Bozeman—beautiful, sexy women—who showed up at his performances, who gave him their number, and yet he couldn't break through the barrier he had placed between himself and the rest of the world to give any of them an honest try. His college girlfriend had been his last serious relationship. He'd loved Mia; she had been tall, with a tan, thick blond hair and a great athletic body. He'd been the envy of all of his friends because he had landed a babe like

Mia. And she had more than looks—she was smart as hell to boot. A straight-A student, bound for law school after they graduated. They had stayed together during all of his many deployments, even though she had told him that he was distant and cold and *different* after he returned from his first tour. When he came home with his back torn up from shrapnel and blast burns, and a purple heart for being wounded in combat, and he *still* wanted to keep on fighting for the cause, that was the end for Mia.

Shane took care of Recon and Top and then he took his guitar outside. It was one day shy of a full moon and he loved to turn off the outside lights on his apartment and play in the soft buttery light of the moon. He strummed the guitar lightly, stopping every now and again to figure out a chord he wanted to play. These were the moments when inspiration for new songs struck—at night, in his little private courtyard world. During a pause in playing, Shane heard the distinct sound of the back porch screen door squeaking shut. He'd thought about oiling those hinges, but then he wouldn't be tipped off when Rebecca came out to hear him play. In all the times she had listened to him from her back porch stairs, she had never asked to join him. Perhaps that was his job.

"Rebecca." He was shrouded by the dark as he approached the back porch. He could see the white T-shirt she had been wearing, but it was difficult to see much else with the roof blocking the light from the moon.

"Hi," she whispered because the boys were in bed now.

He walked over to where she was sitting on the top porch step. "Come sit with me."

He held out his hand to her; even in the sparse light, he knew she could see it.

"No," she whispered. "I don't want to bother you."

"You're not bothering me." He reoffered his hand. "You're inspiring me."

After a second of thought, Rebecca slipped her hand into his. No matter how innocent the moment, it felt so good, so right, to hold Rebecca's hand. There was an instinct in him to find a way to hold on to her hand and never let it go. She slipped her hand free of his and fell in beside him, her arm brushing against his as they walked into the moonlight.

"Don't move," he said. "I'll grab a chair for you."

"Can't we just sit in the grass?"

Shane smiled as he often did around her. "Well, all right, hippy child."

They sat cross-legged on the grass, taking in the sweet smell of Aunt Ginny's rosebushes, which were beginning to bloom.

"I like how quiet it is here," Rebecca said in her smooth, steady voice that he had grown to love. "It reminds me of home."

"You're home now."

She laughed softly, picking at the grass. "I suppose I am."

They didn't speak for a moment or two and then Shane built up the nerve to broach a topic that both of them seemed to be reluctant to broach.

"I suspect that I owe you an apology, Rebecca."

"For?"

"I tied one on pretty good the other night."

Her nod affirmed that she agreed with that characterization.

"You might want to slow down."

His shoulders tensed. She hadn't said anything that hadn't already gone through his mind, but hearing from someone else *again* always set his teeth on edge.

"I've slowed down quite a bit." He fought to keep the tension he felt in his shoulders from seeping into his voice. "But every now and again, it gets away from me."

"You don't have to apologize to me for that." Rebecca pulled her legs up to her chest, wrapped her arms in front of her shins and rested her chin on her knees. The air was still for the most part, but every once in a while, a gentle breeze would dust over them, gently rustling Rebecca's loose mahogany curls. He stared at her profile. He'd never met anyone quite like Rebecca Adams. She was all heart and goodness and positive thinking. But she also had a metal to her character, and a strength the depths of which, Shane believed, Rebecca didn't even know.

"I wanted you to have a good time and I feel like I ruined it for you."

"But you didn't." She lifted her head and stared up at the moon. "I had a wonderful time. I met part of your family, I spent time with Savannah and I got to hear you sing."

She put her hand on his hand for the briefest of moments. "That song that you wrote? I have no idea what you think I did to make your life better, but you made my life better by singing that song for me. I cried all the way through it. And that night, I cried some more just thinking about how beautiful those words were. No one has ever done anything like that for me, Shane. There isn't anything you could have done to ruin it for me."

"You and your boys have been a light that has lit the way for me to dig myself out of a very dark hole."

Rebecca turned toward him so she could look into his face. "I know there's so much I don't know about you, Shane. I know there's so much that you keep bottled up inside. But I also know that you are a good man, a kind man, a man with a heart of gold. I hope one day you'll tell me why your life has been so dark. Sometimes, just speaking the words out loud can be empowering."

The conversation ended there, and he was grateful for it. Those words—his story, his pain—seemed to bubble up when Rebecca was around. Shane felt like an active volcano, just waiting to erupt and let his demons out into the light. He wanted to talk to Rebecca in a way he hadn't wanted to talk to anyone in years. But he just couldn't. He just *couldn't*.

He walked her to the back porch steps, wishing that the night wasn't ending. Wishing that he could follow her into her bedroom and lie down beside her. It didn't even have to be sexual. He just wanted to be near her. The old Shane wouldn't have given Rebecca a second glance. It could be argued that she was cute, but many might consider her to be plain. For Shane, she had become one of the prettiest women he'd ever known. It had started with her eyes, the windows to her pure, sweet soul. He had fallen in love with those eyes. And, now he knew, without any doubt, that he had fallen in love with the rest of the woman.

"Rebecca?"

"Yes?" She turned on the bottom step, her arms crossed in front of her to stave off the night chill that was in the air.

"There's something that I regret."

"Oh, Shane. Please. No more regrets. No more apologies."

"I regret that you might think, even for a moment, that I don't remember our first kiss."

He heard Rebecca breathe in quickly, hold the breath and then let it out slowly.

Shane wrapped his arms around her waist, lifted her off the step and slowly put her down on the ground in front of him.

His lips hovering just over hers, he said, "I remember everything about that kiss, Rebecca."

This time, he kissed her like a man in love. He gently danced his tongue along her lips until she let him in so he could deepen the connection between them. She was stiff in his arms, but she didn't pull away. She wrapped her arms around his waist, lifted up on her toes and tilted her head back as he explored her lips and her mouth, reveling in the taste of her, reveling in the feel of finally having her in his arms. When he released her lips and moved to her neck, Rebecca made the tiniest of moans, and that was when the magical bubble that had surrounded the moment popped. Rebecca stepped away from him, and he let her go.

"Shane." His eyes had adjusted to the dim light at the back of the house. He could see that her chest was rising and falling faster, and her heart must be racing, all from his kisses. "I like you so much."

There was a tear in her voice that hit him in the gut.

"It's not just me anymore. Everything I do—every person I choose—impacts, for the better or for the worse, my sons. I can't just get involved with anyone that—" she paused "—that makes me feel the way you do."

He didn't try to touch her because he was afraid that he might scare her away, but he took a step closer to the woman he loved.

"Rebecca. Am I just anyone?"

"No." That one simple word was said with a waver of emotion. "You're not just anyone, Shane."

"Has any other man made you feel the way I do?" He heard a rasp of emotion in his own voice. "Because I haven't felt this way in my whole entire life about any other woman, the way I'm feeling about you right now."

Rebecca placed her hand on his chest, the spot just over his heart.

"No," she admitted in a whisper. "What I feel for you is…different."

Shane pulled her into his arms and hugged her tightly as he buried his face in her neck.

"Then let me love you, Rebecca," he whispered against her warm skin. "Just let me love you."

The kiss on the back porch had opened the door to a playful, secret, more-than-just-friends relationship with Shane. It was innocent and fun—stolen kisses in the dark, holding hands as they silently watched the world go by after the boys were in bed and sweet words spoken between two lonely people. In high school, Shane was the popular kid—a top jock. He wouldn't have even noticed her in the hallway, much less take her to the prom. But now, she was the woman he wanted. And it felt exhilarating. Life in Bozeman seemed to be turning out well for all of them, even Carson, who received regular baseball lessons from Shane and who was chomping at the bit to try out for a summer little league team. The trips to the baseball field had become a family out-ing of sorts—they always stopped for dinner afterward and, if Carson and Caleb had finished their homework, ice cream. It was a tradition that they all enjoyed.

Rebecca was enjoying her new job and slowly building a regular clientele, the boys' grades were good and she was in love. Perhaps she hadn't admitted it out loud to anyone, but she knew it was true. Shane was kind and talented, and he treated Carson and Caleb like kings. Yet, even though she knew that her love for Shane was real and genuine, she couldn't allow herself to dive into the deep end with him. Shane could have dark moods that turned him inward and made him shut down and close himself off for a couple of days. And there was the drinking. Yes, he limited his drinking to the nighttime, but she could tell by the number of bottles and cans in the recycling bin that the *number* hadn't diminished. He was simply drinking the same amount in a shortened window of time. That didn't seem like an improvement. And it worried her. It worried her enough that she felt that she needed to broach the subject with him before she could take the next step with this man. And, after kissing and petting, Rebecca's body was more than ready to take that next step with Shane.

"Where did you go just then?" Shane's voice shattered her daydreaming and brought her back to the present.

Behind her sunglasses, she smiled at him. "I was just thinking about moving to Bozeman. I had no idea if it would work out for us."

They were lounging on cushions at the front of Gabe Brand's boat; Shane had borrowed his brother's truck, boat and boat trailer, and took them all on an adventure to a nearby lake for Caleb's birthday. Caleb loved to fish, and he'd missed fishing with his father back in New Hampshire.

"Any regrets?"

"No." She gave a slight shake of her head. "I wanted us to have a fresh start."

The boys were fishing off the back of the boat. Rebecca had decided to keep their relationship, as fragile and new as it was, between them. That meant no kissing or hand-holding in front of Carson and Caleb. Shane understood and agreed. Neither of them knew where this was heading exactly and there was no sense disrupting the status quo with her sons.

Shane leaned on his side, his eyes hidden by his mirrored sunglasses, a bottle of water in his hand.

"What happened with their father?"

He had never asked her about her past relationships, and she had never asked him about his.

"Nothing, really."

"Something had to've happened or you would still be married."

"Do you really want to know this?"

"I want to know about you. That's a part of you."

She wondered if she could use that same line on Shane to get him to talk about a past he kept locked away from her.

"Well, I met Tim in the grocery store. He was an assistant manager and I was just a customer returning expired yogurt that I had just purchased. I was a single mom and every penny counted."

"You mean Carson?"

She nodded. "Tim isn't Carson's biological father. He adopted him after we got married."

Rebecca answered the unasked question she saw in

Shane's eyes about her eldest son's biological father when she added, "I wasn't married to Carson's dad and we were so young when I had him—barely adults, really. He couldn't handle the responsibility and I decided that I'd rather make it on my own than force him to do something he wasn't ready to do."

Shane nodded and then waited for her to continue.

"So, it was just Carson and me against the world for a long time and I thought it might be that way forever. But, then, Tim gave me a refund for that expired yogurt and, when he asked for it, I gave him my number."

She shifted her legs to a more comfortable position. "I know it's hard to believe now—" she posed her arms and lifted her chin facetiously "—but I didn't have a lot of dating options back then."

"You're beautiful to me," he interjected quietly so the boys wouldn't hear.

His compliment made her pause and then she continued. "Tim was solid, he was steady, he was—*is*—a great father and provider. We have so much in common."

"Sounds perfect."

"It does. But it wasn't." She tucked some curls behind her ear. "That's what I mean by *nothing* happened. It wasn't a big fight or infidelity or anything dramatic at all. One day he came home and said that he was getting a promotion and they were transferring him to a store in California. We sat at the kitchen table together and he asked, 'Do you want to come with me?' And I said no. And I asked him, 'Do you want me to come with you?' And he shook his head. The only thing that kept us together for the years that we sleepwalked through our marriage was Carson and Caleb. It's not perfect for them—I get that. But they video chat with their father almost every night and they'll see him for Thanksgiving, so…" She shrugged and then, after a moment of thought, she added, "Looking back at it now, I don't think that we were ever in love with each other. We did love each other as people, but I think we *settled* for each other. I don't intend to ever settle again."

"Mom! Shane!"

Caleb's shout for them abruptly ended the conversation. Shane gave her a hand up and they both rushed to the back of the boat in time to see Carson helping Caleb land the biggest catch of his life.

"Mom! Look!"

Shane and Carson took charge of the fish while Rebecca picked Caleb up. She hugged and kissed him on the cheek.

"Happy birthday, my wonderful son." She laughed. "Happy birthday!"

Shane had broken out his grill and fried Caleb's fish for dinner. Spending this family time with Rebecca and her boys made him realize how much he had missed out on not having his own kids. He was still a young man; he hoped that there would be a chance for him to have children of his own. And if it happened with Rebecca, that wouldn't hurt his feelings one bit. Shane had just finished cleaning the grill when he heard the familiar sound of the squeaky back porch screen door. As it always did, his pulse quickened at the thought of being about to hold Rebecca, to kiss Rebecca. He understood why she wanted to keep their shift in status a secret for now. She was a protective mama bear. But this sneaking around in the dark couldn't last forever.

At some point, Rebecca was going to have to decide to claim him as her own. Out of the darkness, his love appeared, wearing a simple cotton shift dress, her face framed by curls, her feet bare. In the courtyard, Rebecca twirled around, her arms out, her head back. He could see that she was happy with how Caleb's first birthday in Montana had gone.

Wordlessly, they took each other's hands and stepped back into the shadows. Her lips were so soft and willing as he intertwined his tongue with hers, holding her tightly. Through her thin cotton dress, he could feel the curves of her body, her full breasts that he ached to kiss. The curve of her thighs just below was where he wanted to bury his body into hers. His hands moved down to her apple bottom, cupped the cheeks and pulled her even closer. He knew that she could feel his arousal; he wanted her to feel it. He wanted her in a way he hadn't wanted a woman in years. And Rebecca wanted him, he was sure of it. But she was afraid of wanting him. She was afraid of what that would mean.

His teeth grazed the silky skin of her neck, moving down to kiss the mound of her breast, wishing he could strip the dress off her body so he could taste her skin and pull her nipple into his mouth. Rebecca made the tiniest, sexiest gasp, swayed her hips toward his groin and dug her fingers into his shoulders.

"Come to my bed," he pleaded with her in a harsh whisper.

Rebecca's breath had quickened and he could feel the tension in her body. She needed him as much as he needed her right now. She dropped her head down and leaned it on his chest.

"I can't, Shane." He heard the conflict in her voice.

"What if one of them wakes up and I'm not there? I can hear them if I'm here. I can see a light turn on, but I can't from inside of the apartment."

Shane groaned in frustration. He kissed her instead of responding, his hands sliding from the hem of her dress up to the top of her thighs.

"At least let me touch you," he said against her lips.

He spun her around and took her deeper into the shadows, a spot in their private oasis, free of prying eyes and listening ears. The ancient trees and the overgrown vines on the hedges protected them by the fact that there was only a sliver of moon in the sky. In the dark, he felt her more than he could see her, his eyes slowly adjusting. But he didn't need to see her. Not for this. He kissed her deeply and slipped his hand inside of her cotton panties.

"Rebecca."

He cupped her, holding her body tight as her knees seemed to buckle at his touch. She was ready for him; all of his thoughts were confirmed with that one touch. She was as hot for him as he was for her.

"Rebecca with the pretty eyes."

Shane slipped his fingers inside of her; she didn't make a sound, but her head dropped to his shoulder and she dug her nails into his arm as she held on. A moment like this had never been so quiet for him; it was more sensual, more intimate, when it was quiet. The only sound was their breaths as he moved inside of her, worrying the most sensitive nub with this thumb. Rebecca tightened her grip on his arm and gasped; he felt her body constrict and pulse around his fingers as he supported her with his free arm. When it was over, he kissed her. He had given her the release that he knew she desperately needed; his body was still aching with it.

"I love you, Rebecca." He rested his chin on her head. "But how much longer can we go on like this?"

Chapter Eight

"Okay. Try it now."

Shane was on his back underneath her kitchen sink, patching a leak.

She turned on the faucet and let the water flow down the drain. "Is it fixed?"

He slid out from underneath the sink with a nod. "It'll hold until I can replace the whole pipe. This house is going to need a plumbing overhaul in the not-too-distant future. I hate to tell you that."

"Well, at least I can still use it. No kitchen sink would be a real pain."

Shane washed his hands and dried them while she put all of the stuff that had been stored under the sink back into place. It was Monday and the boys were at school. She usually worked on Mondays, but the leak in the kitchen had changed her plans. Not working on weekends was cutting into the money she could make, but she hadn't found the right sitter for Carson and Caleb. Jessie did a great job, but she was a busy high school student with a full social life; she wasn't available every weekend. Shane's schedule was too erratic— he played gigs late into the night and often slept late in the morning. And, in the back of her mind, there was the drinking that made her hesitate. Summer was coming and she was going to have to find a solution fast.

Shane sneezed three times in a row and his eyes were swollen with allergies. She handed him a tissue.

"Top slept on you last night?"

He nodded. "I woke up and she was sleeping across my neck like a scarf."

He blew his nose, sounding stuffy when he talked.

"I'll be glad when you finally get to see that allergist."

Shane, she had discovered, didn't like to go to the doctor.

"My appointment's coming up."

"Finally." She knew from experience with her father that wait times for an appointment with the VA could be long.

Rebecca found herself staring at Shane's hands; those hands had given her such pleasure in a stolen moment. The intensity, the passion, the *experience* Shane brought to the table was a strong aphrodisiac to her. The first guy who paid attention to her, a heavyset young man who worked at the local feed store, had a rather severe acne problem and an allergy to spermicide. This was Carson's father. When he found out she was pregnant, he cried. He was more than willing to let Tim adopt Carson, not because he didn't love the boy—she believed that he had—but for the mere fact he wasn't ready to be a father, emotionally or financially. Tim, on the other hand, had been solid as a rock and ready for fatherhood. As a lover, he was polite, cautious and rarely touched her below the waist. Their sex had been routine, quick and always in the missionary position. Whenever she asked if they could "change it up," Tim would lose his erection; eventually, the marriage became sexless, and neither one of them missed it. Rebecca had thought that maybe, even though she was still young, those days of sexual desire were over for her. But Shane had brought her libido back in force. Now she had a secret smile on her face while she worked, and when she went to bed at night, she imagined what it would be like to let Shane make love to her.

"Are you okay?" he asked her.

"Just thinking."

"About?"

"You look like you've lost weight."

"That's what you were thinking?"

She nodded.

He ran his hand over his stomach. "I may have dropped a few pounds. I couldn't have a fifth grader kicking my butt running the bases, so I've been getting some exercise in. I threw away my cigarettes, too."

"Carson will be happy to hear that."

The conversation lulled between them; there was something Rebecca wanted to discuss with Shane. Two things, actually. A discussion about her concerns about his late-night drinking was long overdue, and a discussion about their secret passion was also overdue. The night in the shadows, when Shane had touched her in such an intimate way, she had planned on speaking with him about his drinking. But passion had taken over. It was easier to be kissed by Shane than it was to bring up a touchy subject.

"Do you have a minute to talk?"

They moved to the couch and Rebecca clasped her hands together and put them on top of her thighs.

"If I'm reading this body language, I'm not going to like what you have to say."

Whenever Shane was concerned or thoughtful, he scratched his fingers through his beard and rubbed his jaw. He was doing that now.

"There's something that I've wanted to talk to you about for a while now. I just didn't know how."

"Whatever it is, Rebecca, you just need to spit it out. I see you bite your tongue all the time, when you really should be speaking your mind."

"Give it to you straight?"

A nod.

She took a breath in and after she let it out, her courage gathered and she said, "I think you have a drinking problem, Shane."

His bright blue eyes darkened and his face tensed as he digested her words. "That's not what I thought you were going to say."

He stood up and walked to the center of the living room.

"What do you think about what I *have* said?"

"I don't consider it a problem. I've cut way back. If I had a problem, would I be able to do that?"

His voice rose in volume and she knew that she had struck a sensitive nerve. "Could you just come back here and talk to me?"

Shane sat back down but not as close as he had been.

"I never told you the whole truth about my father. I told you he was a veteran, but what I didn't tell you is that he drank. Not all the time, but too much for my mom to handle. She left Kelly and me to deal with him while she went down to Florida to work as a waitress in a resort. That's where she met Arthur. That's a story for another day."

"What does this have to do with me?" Shane asked, stony faced.

"Everything," she said. "I loved my father and I watched him drown out his memories with alcohol. It hurts me to watch you do the same thing."

He didn't say anything for a moment, his nostrils flaring as he took in deep breaths.

She put her hand on his leg. "I want to have a man in my life, Shane. Someone who loves Carson and Caleb, someone I can grow old with. Maybe even have another baby."

He didn't look at her.

"But I have to be able to trust that man with my sons."

Shane brushed her hand off his leg and stood up. Without a word, he walked stiffly to the door. At the door, he paused.

Not looking at her, he said, "I would never do anything to hurt you or your boys. If you don't know that by now, Rebecca, we are further apart on this thing than I thought."

Hands clenched into fists, Shane marched across the courtyard to his apartment. Recon and Top were waiting for him and they joined him on the couch, comforting him with their affection. Top, who had grown into a lanky teenager and was a week away from being fixed, sprawled across his lap and purred; Recon sat next to him, enjoying a scratch of the thick fur around his neck.

"She's making me feel nuts," he muttered to his four-legged companions.

As far as he was concerned, he didn't have a drinking problem—he had a sleeping problem. He drank so he could fall asleep. He drank enough so that, when he did sleep, it was often dreamless. Ever since the blast that landed him in the hospital, all of his dreams have turned into nightmares.

"What does she want from me?" he asked Recon. "I don't drink during the day anymore. I hardly drink when I play a gig. I never drink around her boys."

A soft knock made Recon bark, jump off the couch and jog to the door, with Top following closely behind. Shane didn't get up. The only person it could be was Rebecca, and he didn't know if he wanted to speak with her at the moment.

"Shane?" Another knock.

"Come in."

Rebecca opened the door and greeted Recon and Top. She picked up the cat and Top rubbed her whiskers all over Rebecca's chin.

"What a big girl you are." Rebecca kissed the young cat and then set her down gently on the ground.

"So, you made me chase you down?" She walked the short distance to where he was sitting with his arms crossed on the couch.

He didn't trust himself to speak, so he remained quiet.

"Okay." She sat down next to him. Now Rebecca was on one side of him, Recon was on the other side and Top had jumped back onto his lap. He was, for all intents and purposes, surrounded.

"That was a hard thing for me to say to you, Shane." When he looked at her, her big pretty eyes were clear and steady. "If I didn't care about you so much," she said, putting her hand on his arm, "I wouldn't have told you the truth."

He swallowed hard. That was the first time Rebecca had said the words that he felt were in her heart: she loved him.

"I feel like I'm falling for you, Shane." He saw the sincerity in her eyes.

He cleared his throat. "I feel the same way about you."

"I see the way you are with Carson and Caleb, and I can't help but hope that one day we could all be a family..."

He'd been thinking a lot about that lately. He wanted to be a husband and a father; Rebecca was the kind of mother he would want for any child of his. The thought of asking Rebecca to marry him, sometime down the road, had crossed his mind several times.

"But—" her eyebrows drew together "—I need you to work some things out, Shane. If it were just me in this, it would be different."

"I'm not going to say that I'll never have another drink," he told her honestly. "But I can promise that I'll think about what you've said."

She leaned over and kissed him on the cheek and then rested her head on his shoulder. "All right."

Having Rebecca this close to him, smelling her hair and her skin, feeling her breath on his neck, triggered thoughts of lovemaking in Shane's mind. Rebecca lifted up her head and looked into his eyes.

"Carson and Caleb won't be home from school for hours," he reminded her.

A pink blush tinged Rebecca's cheeks. In the dark, she could be a vixen, but in the light, she was very shy about her sexuality.

"There's a lot to do around the house," she said.

"A lot." He kissed her on the neck.

"There's laundry I could get done."

He gently bit her earlobe and he felt her shiver with pleasure.

"Dishes to put away."

Before she could continue with her list of mundane chores, Shane kissed her to stop her from saying another word. He unbuttoned her blouse, one button at a time, until the swell of her breasts were exposed.

"Come here." He patted his lap.

Rebecca's eyes widened and it made him laugh.

"Come here," he repeated gently as he showed her what he wanted. Rebecca hesitated, but she straddled him and sat down on his legs.

Shane opened his arms to her and she pressed her body into his. He wrapped her up in his arms, hugging her tightly, as if she would disappear if he didn't hold on tight. Maybe she didn't mean to do it, but she moved her hips and he got so hard it hurt. He took her hips in his hands and moved her back and forth, wanting to bust through his pants and bury himself inside of her. Rebecca sat up; her eyes were closed, her head bent, her hands holding her steady on his shoulders. He watched her face, a face that he had grown to love, while he slowly moved the thin material of her bra down until her nipple was exposed.

Perhaps he should have gone slower, but he couldn't resist taking that nipple into his mouth. Rebecca made a noise and pushed her groin down into his. But then she pulled away and covered her breast.

"What's wrong?"

"I can't do this."

His head dropped back and he closed his eyes, feeling like he was going to live in permanent sexual frustration with this woman.

"Rebecca..."

"They're watching us," she said under her breath, as if Recon and Top could understand her. "I can't do *this* with an audience."

Relieved, Shane laughed. In one motion, he stood up with her still in his arms. She hooked her legs around his hips while he carried her into the bedroom and kicked the door shut. They fell together onto the mattress; Shane's leg was over hers as he looked down into her face.

"You're a beautiful woman, Rebecca."

She turned her head away from him. "Don't say that."

He took his finger and brought her eyes back to his. "You're beautiful."

Not wanting her to object again, he kissed her long and hard. He put all of his love into that one kiss, wanting her to feel all the emotions she had stirred in him that he had only been able to express in his music until now. This woman—this quirky, unusual, unexpected woman—had brought him back to life from the living dead.

Shane stood up and pulled his T-shirt over his head and dropped it on the floor. Rebecca watched him, her eyes appreciating and nervous. Rebecca didn't follow his lead and start to disrobe; he was down to his boxers and she was holding her blouse shut with one hand.

"Turn around," she said.

He looked at her strangely.

She raised her eyebrows and titled her head. "I'm serious. Turn around."

"I want to see you."

"It's the middle of the day," Rebecca said. "Turn around."

"Are you telling me that you've only made love at night?"

"Don't judge."

He did as he was told and turned his back to her while she disrobed. He heard her yank back the covers and the squeak of the loose spring in his mattress as she got into his bed.

"Okay." She said, "You can turn around."

Her clothing was folded neatly on top of his dresser, and Rebecca had the covers pulled up to her chin.

"Don't laugh at me." She frowned at him. "Not all of us are worldly."

Shane would have normally stripped off those boxers, but he decided to keep them on as he joined her in bed. He was going to have to take it slow with Rebecca; she was a mother of two, but seemed to be naive about lovemaking in general. There was so much he wanted to show her. There was so much pleasure he wanted to give to her. That thought, as he took Rebecca into his arms, perked up his waning arousal. Beneath the covers, Rebecca still had her bra and her panties on.

"You planning on keeping these on?" He hooked his finger beneath her bra strap.

"Maybe."

He smiled down at her. "Not a chance."

He kissed her until she forgot about hiding her body from him; he kissed her on her neck and her lips and her ear. He pulled the covers over his head and, with her laughing as he tickled her with his beard, he kissed her belly and thighs while he tugged her panties off. He dropped a kiss at the apex of her thighs, but didn't push the issue of a more intimate kiss. He would save that delicacy for later.

Shane covered her body with his, lying between her thighs, the material of his boxers the only thing that was stopping him from the ecstasy of entering the woman he loved. He suckled her hard nipple through the material of her sensible underwire bra, slipping one strap down her arm and then the other.

With one arm, he lifted her up and unhooked her bra in an easy motion. Her bra was off her body and on the floor before she could think twice about it. His eyes took her in; she had the body of a woman who had borne children—the breasts were full and gravity had made them fall, and she had wider hips and thicker thighs—and all Shane could think was how sexy it was to be in bed with a real woman.

He put his hand on her face, wanting her to see in his eyes that he appreciated what he saw. "Beautiful Rebecca."

She kissed his hand and then wrapped her arms around his back and buried her face in his neck. But he wouldn't let her hide from him. He massaged her breasts, suckling at each nipple while she clung to him silently. She was so quiet in her pleasure, this woman of his. It was almost unnerving. With his lips on her breast, he slipped his hand between her thighs, pleased at how wet she was for him. He cupped her and played with her and stimulated her until she was silently begging, with her hips and her hands, for him to relieve the ache in her body.

Shane yanked off his boxers, not caring that she hadn't touched him. There would be plenty of time for her to explore his body when she became more comfortable with lovemaking in general. All he cared about now was pleasing Rebecca; pleasing her so much that she would want to come back to him for more. He fumbled for a condom in the nightstand drawer, ripped it open with his teeth and slid it on.

He was hovering above her, his arms straight, his hips flush with hers. "Is this what you want, Rebecca?"

Shane didn't want her to have any regrets.

She opened her eyes, those pretty cat's eyes, and he was transported back to the first day he met Rebecca. Her eyes had pulled him in then as they were pulling him in now.

"This is what I want." Her voice had the sultry tone of a woman on the verge of climax. All he had to do was…

He slipped inside of her until he was as deep as he could go. He stopped moving, gritted his teeth to get under control. He needed to be slow with this woman. He needed to be gentle. Their bodies connected. He brushed her hair away from her face and nibbled on her lips. And then he began to move, taking his time, letting her feel every inch of him as he slid all the way to the edge and then plunged back inside. Every stroke brought a small, almost inaudible gasp from Rebecca. It was difficult for him to tell if he was pleasing her, but then she ran her fingernails down his back and muffled a moan in his shoulder.

Shane hooked his leg and arm under her body, and while they were still connected, he rolled her on top of him. The surprised look on her face made him smile.

"I'm yours, Rebecca." He lifted his hip so she could feel him inside of her in a whole new way. Her eyes widened at the sensation. "Do whatever makes you feel good."

Rebecca reached for the covers, pulled them over her shoulders, lay down on top of him and they rocked together, skin to skin, chest to chest, their breathing the only sound; then he felt, rather than heard, her climaxing. She curled her hips into his and shuddered in his arms, holding on to him as if he were her life raft in a storm. He kissed her eyelids and her cheeks; her chest was rising and falling from the exertion, but she was relaxed now and languid in his arms. Confident that he had pleased her, he rolled her onto her back and allowed himself the luxury of quickening the pace, driving into her while she gasped in pleasure, until he exploded. Rebecca hadn't made a peep, but he roared. If the neighbors were home they might have heard him. This was a release of a lifetime. This was a release of years of loneliness, years of self-imposed celibacy and years of self-recrimination. Without understanding how or why, in the arms of Rebecca with the pretty eyes, he had been able to let go of some of the pain he'd been holding on to for so long.

Chapter Nine

Rebecca had never lain in the arms of her lover *post-coitus* in the afternoon. Tim usually got up, immediately took a shower and put on his pajamas after nighttime-only sex. She felt naughty and decadent and definitely wanted more afternoons just like this. Shane was lying on his back, his breathing steady, while he absentmindedly twisted her curls around one of his fingers. She had her head on his chest, her fingers combing through the light brown chest hair, feeling secure in his arms and comforted by the strong beat of his heart.

"I don't even know your middle name," she murmured.

"Alexander."

"Shane Alexander Brand," Rebecca said. "Such a strong name."

"Alexander was my grandfather. On my mother's side."

"That's funny. My middle name is in honor of my father's mother. Her name was May."

"Rebecca May." Shane sounded as if he was drifting in and out of sleep.

"Shane?"

"Hmm?"

"Tell me something I don't know about you?"

He stretched his arm, flexed his fingers and then hugged her more tightly to his body. He looked down at her, meeting her eye.

"Like what?"

"Something. Anything. But it has to be important. It can't be something like your favorite color."

"Red."

"Other than that."

When he didn't answer, she poked him on the chest with her finger.

"I'm thinking."

She kissed his neck while she waited, and he tightened his grip on her again. "You keep on doing that and we won't be doing any talking at all."

"Tell me."

"Okay." He rubbed his hand over his face several times. "Something you don't already know about me." Shane was quiet for such a long time that Rebecca was beginning to think that he wasn't going to answer. Then, after a sigh, he said in a low, solemn voice, "Okay. Something that you might not know about me is Recon wasn't always my dog."

She waited for him to continue; they seemed to be so connected, she had always assumed that Shane had raised Recon from a puppy.

Shane was staring straight ahead, a far-off look in

his eyes, blinking as if he were trying to blink away his emotions.

"Recon," he finally continued, "belonged to my best friend, Dustin."

Rebecca curled her body around so she was facing him with the sheet covering her breasts. Shane had spoken about Dustin before, telling Carson baseball stories after they practiced. "Your catcher?"

Shane nodded. "He was so talented, that kid. More talented than me by a mile."

Instinctively, she reached out and took his hand in hers as he continued.

"We're both in college on scholarships. Dustin's brother, Jeff, gets killed in Iraq and next thing I know, Dustin's gung-ho to sign up to fight. I couldn't—" Shane paused for a moment before he continued "—I couldn't just keep on going to classes while my best friend was in that fight. He joins the marines. I join the army."

He hadn't said the words yet, but she knew what he was about to say. She felt it in her gut. There was another pregnant pause and she watched Shane swallow hard several times, and she felt he was always so determined to push down any feelings that might cause him more pain.

"I made it back alive." There was an angry catch in Shane's voice. "Dustin came back in a body bag." His free hand balled into a fist. "We couldn't even have a damn open casket at his funeral."

She squeezed his hand because saying she was sorry seemed so trite and insignificant.

"Recon was too much for his parents to handle

long-term—they're older and he can be a handful—so
I agreed to take him."

He had been staring at the wall, but now linked his
eyes with hers. "Now you know the story about Recon
and me."

As if on cue, the moment was interrupted by a
scratching at the door. Rebecca turned her head toward the door and saw a black arm attached to a white
paw under the door. It was exactly the moment of levity they needed after Shane revealed such a personal
and painful part of his past.

Shane propped himself up on his elbow and laughed.
"She cracks me up, that cat."

Rebecca turned back to the man she had just spent
the afternoon loving. She put her hand on his chest.
"Thank you, Shane. For telling me about Dustin."

"It's hard to talk about him." Shane kept his eyes on
the door. "I miss him like crazy. Every day."

They both knew that their late-morning tryst had to
end; Rebecca *did* have chores that needed to be done
before Carson and Caleb got home. And Shane had a
gig that night and needed some time to prepare. She let
Shane get up first, holding the sheet and blanket tightly
against her body. He sat on the edge of the bed and it
was the first time she had ever seen Shane's back. She
knew that the skin had felt different to the touch, but
to see it, in the light of day, was a different thing entirely. Most of his back was scarred, some from burns
and the rest from, she assumed, shrapnel or bullets. She
clutched the sheet with her hand to stop herself from
reaching out to touch the scars, to stop herself from saying anything to him about them. He'd already opened
up more just a moment ago than he had ever in the time

she had known him. It didn't seem like a good idea to push him. But once she got a good look at the physical scars that Shane carried, it gave Rebecca some insight into the emotional scars the man must carry, as well. It must be a heavy, nearly unbearable burden.

Shane stood up, naked as the day he was born, and stretched his arms above his head before he pulled on his boxers. He turned around, smiled at her like a man who had been well satisfied in bed and scratched his chest and then his beard.

"You need another trim," she observed.

"Do you know anybody who could help me with that?" He winked at her.

"Would you ever consider shaving that beard off?"

His hand went to his face protectively. "Not a chance."

"Okay." She waved her hand at him. "Go out there and shut the door so I can get dressed."

"Are you serious? I just kissed you all over that beautiful body of yours." He put his knee on the bed and leaned toward her. "As a matter of fact, I think I want seconds."

He started playfully kissing on her neck and laughing, but she pushed him away. "Quit it! I've got to get dressed."

Shane dressed quickly, left the room and shut the door as she had requested. Rebecca grabbed her bra off the floor and then had to search in the bedclothes to find her discarded panties.

"Hussy," she said with a smile on her face.

Once she was dressed and her hair, which was wild from the lovemaking, was semi-tamed, she met Shane outside. Recon and Top were in the courtyard, enjoying the fresh air.

"I wish I could come to the show tonight." She tucked her hands in the back pocket of her jeans.

"I'll miss you." He looked her way. "Your shirt is buttoned wrong."

She looked down and her shirt was crooked because she had the buttons in the wrong holes.

She rolled her eyes and crossed her arms to hide the shirt. "I suppose I was overdue for a walk of shame. Lucky for me, it's a very short distance."

They gave each other a quick kiss goodbye and then Rebecca walked quickly to her back porch.

"Carson has tryouts tomorrow," he reminded her.

From the back porch, she answered. "I know. I'm so nervous for him."

"Don't be. He's going to kill it."

Rebecca looked forward to Monday mornings all week long. The boys were in school and it was the time when she could be free to spend time with Shane, not as a mom, but as a woman. It had become their routine for Shane to come over in the morning for coffee and breakfast and then, inevitably, they found their way to her bedroom. Looking back on her past romantic encounters, Rebecca realized that her prior lovers truly did not know the many ways a man could make a woman's body hum. And now she was bolder, more willing to experiment or be in charge. She certainly had lost much of her shyness, not minding at all being naked in front of Shane. He liked her curves—he appreciated being with a woman with some "meat on her bones." He made her feel beautiful, and what woman wouldn't like that?

"That was wonderful," she said dreamily of their lovemaking.

Even though she didn't have her eyes open, she knew that he was smiling. He was propped up on the pillows, one arm behind his head, the other holding on to her while she, as she liked to do, rested her head just above his strongly beating heart.

"When am I going to get to take you out on a real date, Rebecca?"

This wasn't the first time Shane had brought up this topic. He was ready to take their relationship public and she just wasn't there yet. Realizing that her blissful moment of lying naked next to her man, languid and decadent and high on lovemaking endorphins, was about to come to an end, she stopped running her fingers through his chest hair, prepping for the disagreement to come.

"What's the rush, Shane?" she asked. And she meant it. She was happy, for now, with the way things were.

She liked that she had part of her life that was only for her, when so much of her life was focused on being the best mother she could be. Their romance was still new, still fresh and still a secret. She was a great mother, a good provider—shouldn't she have something just for her that made her happy? Shane Brand, in spite of his many emotional scars, made her feel happy. The thought of Shane, the way his lips felt on her skin, how safe she felt in his arms, would make Rebecca smile when she was at work. Thinking about Shane was her happy place; to bring the boys in now, which would undoubtedly complicate matters, didn't seem appealing to her *at all*.

He sat up, displacing her. "Come on, Rebecca. We're

talking about dinner. In public, God forbid. I wouldn't call that rushing anything. I'm starting to feel like your dirty little secret, and I tell you what—I don't like it."

Rebecca turned away from him, got out of bed, quickly found her underwear on the other side of the room, pulled them on and scooped up her clothes. She held her clothes in front of her body, instead of getting dressed, knowing that she needed to take a shower before work. Shane got out of bed, too, and yanked on his jeans.

"Why did you have to ruin this? We were having such a good time."

His jeans were on but not zipped or buttoned, and his chest was bare. Shane pushed his long hair out of his eyes and she saw that there was a flash of hurt in his aqua-blue eyes.

"*Ruin* this? How did I ruin this?"

"This is supposed to be my time to relax and forget my problems, not add to them."

Shane took a step toward her; she could plainly see, by the look on his face, that this conversation was going to take a different path.

He pointed at his chest. "I'm not an amusement park ride, Rebecca. I'm a man. A man who wants things." He held up his fingers to start ticking off the things that he wanted. "I want a woman to love, who loves me as much as I love her, I want a family, I want to be a father and I want to be a husband. If I just wanted sex, there are plenty of options at my gigs."

This was the first time Shane had alluded to marriage. Her divorce, although a year old, seemed like it happened just yesterday. Even when it was an amicable parting, the legal hoops of divorce, the expense and the tediousness of changing everything, from the cable bill to bank accounts, was an ordeal. Not to mention, most important, the toll it had taken on Carson and Caleb.

Perhaps he saw the deer-in-the-headlights look on her face because he added, "I'm not saying I want to get married tomorrow. I'm saying, let's move our relationship past the bedroom and into a restaurant. Or a movie theater."

When she couldn't think of the right thing to say, he made a frustrated noise and finished zipping up his pants. He turned away from her to grab his shirt off the floor. Silently, he sat on the edge of the bed and put on his boots. Not wanting their time together to end badly, Rebecca sat down next to him on the bed and bumped his shoulder with hers.

"I just need more time, Shane. We have no idea how Carson and Caleb will feel about us dating. They've had so much change in their life, I don't want to throw yet another big thing at them."

"Carson and Caleb and I are buddies. I'd think they'd be happy about it."

She shook her head. "Kids can react funny. Caleb still has trouble with the divorce and sometimes he asks me if Dad can move back in with us. You're our friend right now. If you start dating their mom, it might even change your relationship with them."

Shane seemed to consider her words and then he took her hand in his. "I don't want to do anything to hurt either one of your boys."

"I know you don't."

They sat together on the edge of the bed, each in their own thoughts. Finally, Shane restarted the conversation.

"When I first saw you, I thought, now there's a woman a man could marry."

Rebecca smiled up at Shane, loving it when their eyes met and held.

"My wild oats are sown. I'm ready to settle down." He lifted her hand up and kissed it. "It would be nice if I could settle down with you one day. But the truth is, I don't know what you want from me, Rebecca, because you've never told me. Not once."

She put her free hand on top of his. "I want to be married again. At the right time, to the right man this time. And," she added softly, "I'd like to have another baby. Try for a girl."

He gently brought her face back toward him. "Am I the right man? For you?"

She wanted to say yes. She wanted to reassure him. But the problem was, after one failed marriage, she needed more evidence than chemistry and friendship. She needed to know that they could make it for the long haul.

"I know that I love you, Shane," she said. "I know that you are wonderful with Carson and Caleb."

She looked down at their entwined fingers. "But I also know that I need more time…to figure things out."

Shane lifted her chin up and kissed her on the lips. "I can be a very patient man."

"When you want to be?"

"When I want to be." Shane kissed her neck.

Rebecca loved Shane's kisses; the way he nibbled on her lips, the way he held her in his arms. It was easy to lose her attachment to reality in those moments, pushing away thoughts of leaky pipes and laundry and grocery shopping.

"It's still early," he murmured. His hand had slid beneath her blouse and the palm of his hand massaged the lower part of her back.

A wonderful shiver of anticipation rushed over her; she could see the telltale bulge near Shane's groin. The man had a healthy libido and he liked to make up for their once-a-week trysts by making love to her twice.

Shane tugged her clothing out of her arms, exposing her breasts. Her instinct to hide her body in the dark had diminished and she now felt less embarrassment and more enjoyment when Shane admired her body. And she sincerely enjoyed admiring Shane's transforming body. All of the crunches and push-ups he'd been doing, the beers he'd been bypassing and the cigarettes he'd thrown in the trash had paid off in spades. The man was on his way to being ripped; he had dropped excess pounds and his arms, his abs, his chest were shaping up to be the stuff of female fantasies.

"Lay back."

"Why?"

He looked like a man on a mission and that caught her attention. Shane was much more experienced in the bedroom than she was and he liked to push the boundaries with her comfort zone. From their first encounter in the dark, he had been challenging her to be more adventurous with her sexuality.

He cocked one eyebrow at her at the fact that she was questioning him.

"Have I ever done anything to you that didn't feel good?"

"Not yet," she admitted.

"Not ever." He guided her back gently and then hooked his fingers on the waistband of her panties.

Soon her panties were on the floor again, with the rest of her clothing. This was when he would usually join her in bed. But this time, he didn't.

He knelt down and tugged her legs apart. Caught off guard, Rebecca sat up and pressed her knees together.

"I don't think so."

Tim had tried kissing her down there once and it had been a disaster; he got a cramp in his neck, and maybe he did it wrong, but it kind of hurt. She had felt embarrassed and vulnerable and not sexy at all. It reminded her of a gynecological exam minus the nurse and the cat hanging on a limb "Hang in there!" poster on the ceiling. After that, it had been difficult for Rebecca to understand why any woman would want *that* done to her.

"No?" he asked, disappointed.

She kept her knees pressed together tightly. "The last time someone did…*that* to me, I didn't like it."

Shane gave her a cocky smile. "Darlin', if you didn't like it, he was doing it wrong. An amateur. Do I seem like an amateur to you?"

She frowned at him. "No."

"What's the worst that could happen? If you don't like it, we'll stop."

For some reason, Shane wanted to do *that* to her, and she wanted him to. Maybe he was right—maybe her ex was doing it wrong.

Rebecca held out her finger as if to lay down the law. "Okay. But if I don't like it…"

"Which won't happen."

"But, if I don't."

He leaned forward and gave her a quick kiss on the lips. "You're the boss. Now lie back and let me have some fun."

Rebecca lay back, her eyes closed, her body tense and her arms covering her breasts in an attempt to feel less vulnerable and exposed. Shane was gentle with her, easing her legs apart, rubbing her legs to help her relax. She almost called the whole thing off, but then she felt his beard brush against the inside of her thighs, his warm breath on her skin and then the wonderful feeling of his firm lips as he kissed her in that most sensitive place. Rebecca held her breath, waiting for it to be uncomfortable, but soon all of those doubts and experiences from the past were blasted out of her brain by the sensation of Shane's tongue inside of her. Rebecca arched her back, grabbed the sheets with her hands and bit down hard on her lip to keep from crying out. What had she been missing? *What* had she been *missing*?

"Let me hear you," Shane murmured.

"The kids," she whispered on a gasp.

There were always kids in the next room and she had learned to stifle any noise that she may want to make during sex.

"At school. Let me hear you."

Shane was treating her like his favorite ice-cream cone, sending mini-explosions of pleasure from the core of her body out to her fingertips and her curled toes. And then it happened. So unexpected. So out of character. Shane hit that little nub with the tip of his tongue one more time and she felt that familiar, wonderful tension in her groin roll over her body like an ocean wave, sending lovely tingles dancing across her naked skin. Behind her eyes, Rebecca saw an explosion of colors, like a Fourth of July fireworks display. Her arms outstretched, her head back, completely uninhibited in the moment, Rebecca cried out, as Shane loved her with his mouth. Out of breath, her chest rising and falling quickly, it took Rebecca a moment to reorient to the room. She opened her eyes just a crack and watched Shane roll a condom onto his shaft. He was on the bed and inside of her so quickly that it made her gasp; she was so sensitive, she could feel every hard inch of him.

Not moving, he took her face in his hands. "Now, do I have permission to put that in the regular lineup?"

Suddenly self-conscious, Rebecca felt herself blush. "If you want."

His arms braced so he held himself above her, Shane started to move inside her, his eyes never leaving her face. "Trust me, Rebecca. I want."

Chapter Ten

"I love a baseball game on a sunny afternoon," Savannah said. "Thank you for inviting us."

Rebecca was holding Amanda, who was always fascinated by her curly hair. She would periodically catch the baby girl's eyes and make a face, and that would make Amanda laugh and smile. But most of the time, her eyes were on Carson, who was standing on the pitcher's mound. He looked so mature and handsome in his new uniform. After Shane's intensive coaching, Carson easily made a team sponsored by a local feed store as starting pitcher. She'd never seen her son this excited about anything, and it made her feel grateful to Shane for the interest he had taken in Carson and the time he spent coaching him. This was the first game of the season, and even though it was just a practice game, it was important to her son.

"I'm glad you could come," she said. "I'm so happy that he made the team. He's had a harder time adjusting than Caleb."

She had been keeping a watchful eye on her youngest son, who was using a gap in the chain-link fence around the ball field to take pictures of his brother pitching.

"I just don't know how I'm going to juggle work, little league and having them home for the summer. Back home, I had a pretty long list of childcare options."

"You could always bring them out to the ranch," Savannah suggested after a minute.

Rebecca looked at her friend, surprised.

"There's plenty for them to do out there and plenty of people to watch them," her friend explained. "Bruce would be happy to put them to work."

It was an unexpected solution to her problem; one that seemed worth at least exploring.

"Why don't you bring the boys to Sunday brunch after church—the Brands have a big brunch every Sunday—it's a tradition. That way, you could meet everyone, see that ranch."

She accepted the invitation. It might not be a permanent solution to the problem, but it might be a backup plan if she couldn't find the right childcare solution for the boys during the summer.

"And," Savannah added, "if you could manage to pull off a miracle and drag Shane along with you, the family would probably make you an honorary Brand on the spot."

Rebecca laughed. "I don't have that kind of influence over Shane."

Savannah had a look on her face that let Rebecca know that her friend didn't really believe that statement.

"I think you have more than you think," the young mother said. "I mean, look at him. He's lost weight, he's in better shape—you've managed to get him to tame that out-of-control beard. He actually looks healthy again." Her friend nodded her head toward where Shane was standing near the dugout. Carson's team needed an assistant coach and Shane had agreed to take on the job, which had made her eldest son's baseball triumph that much sweeter for him.

It was true that Rebecca *had* managed to convince Shane to let her trim down his beard and shorten his hair again. He looked less like a mountain man now, and she knew that she could take at least some of the credit for that.

Amanda started to fuss and reach out for her mother; Rebecca passed the baby back to her friend. Savannah bounced Amanda on her knee as she continued. "I know this's none of my business. And if you don't want to answer, I won't be offended. Is there something between you and Shane?"

"Friendship," Rebecca said honestly. They were friends. In fact, Rebecca counted Shane as one of the best friends she'd ever had in her life. The detail she left out? He was a friend who also happened to be her lover.

"Are you…more than friends?"

Rebecca didn't want to lie to her friend, but didn't know what to say.

Savannah filled in the silence. "I only ask because I've seen the way he looks at you…"

"Becca."

"Kelly!" Rebecca said her sister's name with enthusiasm she rarely felt at seeing her younger sibling and waved her to the top of the bleachers, where they had a bird's-eye view of the entire field.

The one thing that Rebecca could say about her sister was that Kelly had perfect timing. She knew when to smile, when to leave, when to throw a sarcastic comment to her father to get him out of a *mood* and she always knew when to arrive. Today was a perfect example; Kelly arrives and Savannah's question about her relationship with Shane fades into the ether like it had never been posed in the first place.

"Your sister is so pretty," Savannah said.

It was true—her sister *was* pretty. And it had been difficult to be the sister who was considered *unremarkable* by most. Kelly slowly ascended the wood-and-metal steps of the bleachers, holding her Hermes bag on the side away from the people occupying the end caps of each bench, as if they might, in some unknown way, harm the overpriced, overly large purse. Kelly lived in Bozeman, but she shopped in New York City, and she always dressed in a power suit on weekdays, in a state where it was acceptable to wear cowboy hats and jeans to weddings and funerals. The diamonds encircling Kelly's wrist and embellishing her ears and fingers sparkled in the waning afternoon sun as she approached.

"Sidney sends his apologies," her sister said as she joined them, perching on the edge of the bleacher.

Kelly's husband, Sidney, had made a financial killing on Wall Street before he decided to quit the "rat race" and become a gentleman Montana farmer. His midlife crisis had brought Kelly to Bozeman, and in perfect Kelly style, she made the best of it, keeping herself busy by becoming the go-to Realtor for the wealthiest of the wealthy.

"Thank you for coming," Rebecca told her sister. "Carson's been warming up. They're just about to start the game, so you haven't missed anything Carson wants you to see."

Kelly pushed her shiny wavy hair away from her face with a nod. "I wouldn't miss this."

Regardless of the friction between the sisters, Carson and Caleb loved their aunt and uncle. For the sake of her sons, Rebecca had to put aside her years of baggage with Kelly and make an effort with her only sibling.

"Do you know Savannah?"

"Certainly." Kelly leaned forward and offered her hand. "But we haven't seen each other for a while. The silent auction, I think?"

Rebecca sent them a questioning look.

"I have a foundation, Sammy Smiles, and we hold events every spring and fall to raise money," Savannah explained.

"I'd love to get involved," Rebecca told her friend. "Let me know if you need help."

Savannah laughed as she brushed her hand over Amanda's fine strawberry blond hair. "We *always* need help."

Rebecca had nearly lost her voice from cheering for Carson so much during the game. She had never seen him play the way he played in this practice game. He was really *good*—six strikeouts in one game. As his mother, she thought he was exceptional. But objectively, after this game, it was undeniable that this kid had an incredible arm. Combined with targeted coaching by Shane, Carson's hard work had paid off in the practice game. Rebecca met her son at the bottom of the bleachers.

"You. Were. Amazing." She hugged him first, and then let him go to his aunt. Carson in particular had bonded with Kelly early on in his life; that bond seemed to be holding regardless of the fact that he didn't see her as much as he wanted.

"Did you see me?" Carson had his expectant face upturned to Kelly.

Kelly hugged him again, her love for her nephew softening the expression on her face. "I saw the whole thing."

Caleb ran up to them, barreling into Kelly's arms, which made her sway back a bit as she absorbed the bear hug from her youngest nephew.

"What in the world do you have all over your face, Caleb?" Rebecca lifted his chin once he let loose of Kelly.

"Shane gave me money to get something to eat."

She tried to rub it off with her thumb. "It's blue. And sticky."

"Cotton candy." Caleb bounced up and down like he was riding a pogo stick.

Rebecca frowned as she brushed her younger son's sweaty hair off his forehead. "You're hot. Do you feel okay?"

Caleb nodded, and Rebecca was distracted for a moment when Savannah interrupted to give her a quick hug. "I have to get Amanda home. She's been so good, but that's not going to last if I don't head out now. I'll call you."

They kissed each other on the cheek and promised

to make plans for a trip out to Sugar Creek after church the following Sunday.

"Well," Kelly said after a pause in the conversation, "I'd better be on my way also."

"Busy day tomorrow?"

"Full calendar." She nodded, checking her phone.

"Say goodbye to your aunt," Rebecca said to Carson and Caleb.

They took turns hugging her goodbye and then Carson said, "We're going to go help Shane with the equipment."

"Okay. But don't forget, it's still a school night."

Carson nodded and then he looked at Kelly. "Don't be a stranger, Aunt Kelly."

They walked together along the sidewalk, being passed by other parents and kids rushing to get home. As was typical, the conversation waned between the sisters. At the end of the sidewalk, they stopped, not facing each other, and Rebecca struggled to find a way to end the interaction, which had been unusually positive, without igniting new friction between them.

"I mean it, Kell. I really appreciate you coming tonight. It meant so much to Carson."

"When I'm invited, I come."

And there it was, right on schedule—a jab. Opting not to punch back, Rebecca took in a steadying breath before she responded. After a pause between them, Kelly changed the topic. "Have you spoken to Mom lately?"

Rebecca shook her head. Her relationship with her mother was strained, with communication being infrequent and often unsatisfying. She knew that she had never quite gotten over her mother leaving them behind to start a new life. Perhaps she never would.

"We got into it again," her sister said, with a hint of satisfaction in her small smile.

Kelly had kept in touch with their mother regularly, and Rebecca believed it was, in part, to dole out punishment for misdeeds of years past. Kelly liked to poke the bear, while Rebecca liked to move far away from the den in an attempt to never see the bear, much less confront it.

"Arthur."

The way Kelly said their stepfather's name, like she had just smelled something rotten in the air, made Rebecca laugh. They both had a meeting of the minds when it came to *Arthur.* Their mother had met her new husband through online dating and she had been effusive in her praise of the man from day one.

"The woman went on and on and on for an hour about how talented Arthur's grandson is at golf. She's convinced that he's the next Tiger Woods, even though he's only five. *Five.*" Kelly rolled her eyes. "Anyway. All I did was ask Mom if *Tiger* was going to walk on water as an encore."

Rebecca laughed again.

"Funny, right?"

"I thought so," Rebecca agreed.

"Then I got the lecture about respecting her marriage, blah, blah, blah. Now she's officially not speaking to me."

"Again?"

Kelly fished her keys out of her purse. "You know she'll call me tomorrow. She can't help herself."

"Why do you guys always have to push each other's buttons?"

"It's how we communicate." Her sister gave her a quick hug. "Text me the details for the next game."

"I will." Rebecca watched her sister reach her car, get in and turn on the engine and lights. Kelly rolled down the driver's-side window and waved her hand. Rebecca cupped her hands over her mouth so her sister could hear her over the noise. "I'm glad you came."

She had said similar things to her sister over the years, mostly out of obligation, politeness or in an attempt to maintain the social facade that their relationship *wasn't* completely dysfunctional. But this time, and much to her surprise, she had actually meant it. Their relationship had been fractured for so many years; it was difficult for Rebecca to know how to repair it. But moments like tonight—at the very least, it was a start.

"Are they asleep?" Shane was waiting for her on a bench he had placed just outside his apartment. He had deliberately positioned it so that at night they would be in the shadow, and therefore he could give her sweet good-night kisses in their own private, romantic garden. Tonight, she could see Top's white body sitting on the bench next to Shane, which meant that she would need to be careful not to accidentally step on Recon, who was surely nearby.

With a sigh, Rebecca sat down next to him and put her head, as she always did, on his shoulder for a moment. "Finally. Carson was so wound up, I had to let him retell his favorite moments from the game one more time before he finally got into bed. Usually I have to fight Caleb to get him in bed, but tonight he was in bed before the first reminder."

She slanted a look at her companion and teased him by saying, "Probably a sugar coma from the cotton candy."

"He said he wanted a hot dog."

Rebecca laughed. "I'm sure he fully intended to get a hot dog—until he saw the cotton candy."

"Can you really blame him?"

"No," she said. "If I were his age and someone handed me a twenty? Cotton candy all the way."

"Me, too," Shane agreed with a laugh. After a moment, he said, "Tonight was a good night."

She took his hand in hers. "Tonight was a *great* night."

Recon moved over to where she was sitting, nuzzled her free hand for a pet, and then, as he liked to do lately, laid his body across her feet possessively. Rebecca rubbed her fingers lightly over the rough skin of Shane's fingers; his hands were so weathered for a man who hadn't yet reached middle age. The hands were rough, with thin white scars on the thumb of his left hand and on the middle finger of his right hand. The skin was often dry, and she would stop him in the middle of chores to put healing lotion on his hands. But they were strong and capable hands. The type of hands a woman could be inclined to count on; hands that a woman could be inclined to hold for the rest of her life.

"I had no idea how good Carson is," she admitted quietly. "No idea."

"He's got the juice."

"I hope this team turns out to be what he needs."

Shane turned his head to look at her, and she could read the question in his body language.

"To fit in," she explained. "Caleb is so easygoing. Everyone loves him—he just flashes those dimples when he smiles and people can't wait to fawn over him. Carson is more…inside of himself. But when he's on that pitcher's mound…"

There was a smile in her voice as memories of her son's performance during the game cycled through her mind.

Shane filled in the rest. "He's in charge."

She nodded. "I've never seen him that way before." She squeezed his hand. "He couldn't have done it without you, Shane."

He squeezed her hand in return, and she knew that this was his way of saying "you're welcome."

After a moment of silence, Rebecca laughed.

"What?"

"I just realized. You haven't sneezed once."

As if she knew that she was being discussed, Top meowed and flopped onto Shane's lap.

"I'm loaded up on new prescription meds, baby." He laughed gently. "The doc at the VA says that I might want to get the shots. Might not be a bad idea."

She leaned into Shane, soaking in the feeling of having his warm body next to hers. "Do you know, the lengths you have gone to give Top a home is one of the many things I love about you, Shane? No matter how bad your allergies got, you wouldn't let her go."

He was quiet for a second. And then he said what he always said about Top. "She's worth it. She's my family now."

* * *

Shane had dozed off on the couch with Top and Recon when an insistent knocking on his door awakened him. He squinted in the dark, trying to orient to the time. He grabbed his phone off the coffee table; it was just after midnight.

"Rebecca?" He stood up and shuffled to the door, wondering why she hadn't just come in. When he got to the door, he remembered that he had locked it behind him.

"Caleb's spiked a fever and I can't break it," Rebecca said urgently. "I'm taking him to the ER."

"Let me get my shoes and I'll meet you at the car."

"I need you to watch Carson," she said in a rush. "He's still conked out. He's so exhausted."

Shane grabbed his socks and shoes and ran over to the main house. Rebecca had bundled Caleb up in a blanket on the couch. Wordlessly, Shane scooped up the boy and carried him to the car. Caleb's skin was hot to the touch; he was burning up and his normally wide, mischievous eyes were closed. Shane settled the boy in the back seat, securing the seat belt around his body in a way that allowed Caleb to curl up on his side.

He met Rebecca at the driver's side.

"I'll text you as soon as I get there."

He nodded and opened the door for her. "Let me know what's going on."

"I will." Rebecca paused, seeming to be conflicted before she got behind the wheel. She looked up into his face, studying him in the light coming from porch. She put her hand on his chest and said, "You're okay, right?"

She didn't have to say out loud what was on her

mind—she wanted to know if he was sober enough to watch Carson.

"I'm fine." He'd only had a couple of beers hours ago.

"Okay." She took a seat behind the wheel. "Promise me you won't drink anything while you're watching him, Shane. I have no idea how long I'll be gone."

"I promise." He frowned at her, frustrated that she even had to question him during an emergency. "Don't worry, Rebecca. I've got this."

Chapter Eleven

Rebecca had left with Caleb to go to the hospital early in the morning, when it was still dark. When she pulled into the driveway, the sun had come up and, according to Shane's last text, Carson had gotten up, gotten dressed, they had eaten a bowl of cereal together and her son had made the bus on time. Caleb, who was finally feeling better after he was treated for an ear infection, was asleep in the back seat. With a tired sigh, Rebecca opened the back-seat door.

"Wake up, little man. We're home."

Caleb walked groggily to the house, the thin white blanket from the hospital still wrapped around his shoulders. Inside the door, Rebecca hugged her son and kissed him on the head.

"Go on and get into bed. I'll bring you something to drink and your medicine in a minute."

Caleb shuffled through the living room, waving his hand weakly at Shane, who appeared to be waking up from dozing off in the reclining chair.

"Are you feeling better?" Shane asked.

"Yeah," her son mumbled before he headed up the stairs.

Rebecca dropped her keys, phone and purse, as well as Caleb's meds, on the coffee table and slumped onto the couch. She rubbed her burning eyes and yawned loudly.

"What a night."

Shane crossed to her side of the room, sat down next to her and gave her hand a quick, reassuring squeeze. He didn't hold on to it, just in case Caleb came back down the stairs. But his close proximity, his presence, made her feel comforted.

"You had to cancel your clients?"

"Yes." She shook her head at the thought of it. She hated canceling, but sometimes it just wasn't avoidable.

"I was able to reschedule all but one person. She's going to see Baily today." Rebecca closed her eyes, feeling as if she could fall asleep sitting up. Her head bobbed forward and she forced herself to open her eyes. Blinking quickly several times, she leaned forward, rested her elbows on her thighs and her head in the palms of her hands.

"I have to get Caleb his medication and then I've got to get some sleep."

Shane stood up and offered her his hand. She accepted the hand gratefully, stood up and gave him a brief hug, wishing she could crawl into bed with Shane and wrap herself in his arms.

"Thank you for watching Carson." She reached for the package of meds. "Any problems?"

"Not one." Shane scratched his fingers through his beard. "That kid's an old young guy, you know?"

She did know. Carson, so many times, seemed mature beyond his years.

"He took care of business and got on the bus. I was just a bystander."

"Well." She sent him a tired smile. "Thank you for being a bystander. He would have missed a day of school if you hadn't been here."

Shane left to take care of Recon and Top while she poured Caleb his favorite flavor of Gatorade in a glass without ice. She was putting the bottle back in the refrigerator when her fuzzy eyes noticed something out of place. At the back of the refrigerator, she had a six-pack of beer that she had purchased months ago; even though the six-pack was still turned in a way that there were still two beers showing in the front, one of the beers was missing from the back part of the six-pack.

The refrigerator door still propped open, Rebecca stared at the missing beer, trying to remember if it had been missing for a while and she just hadn't noticed. Her fingers gripped the handle tightly until it hurt and her stomach felt uncomfortable, not from hunger but from a nagging feeling that something she didn't want to happen or face had in fact happened.

"Mom."

Caleb calling for her snapped her out of her dark thoughts. She ascended the stairs, carrying the glass and meds, fighting a headache. It was a relief that Caleb was feeling well enough to sleep once he took his meds; it was a relief that he was feeling better. In the doorway of her sons' bedroom, she paused and watched Caleb drifting off to sleep. After a moment, she walked quietly down the stairs, careful to avoid the squeaky boards. She had intended to lie down in Carson's bed so she could catch a couple of hours of sleep in ear range of Caleb, but the nagging questions around that missing beer had given her a shot of adrenaline, and with so many thoughts and worries swirling around in her brain, she doubted she could fall asleep now even if she tried.

She found herself standing in front of the refrigerator again, staring at the spot where a sixth beer should be with a wrinkled brow.

"Surely he didn't." Rebecca moved the lettuce and a half-eaten sandwich wrapped in paper towel out of the way, grabbed the six-pack and set it down on the kitchen counter. Leaning back against the sink, she rubbed her finger across her bottom lip in thought. She knew that she hadn't had a beer in months and Carson, who was the only one in the house that could even be a suspect, other than Shane, had never shown a desire or inclination to even try a sip of beer or wine. It had to be Shane. The only thing that she couldn't decide for certain was if he had it last night or some other time when he was at the house.

Annoyed, Rebecca grabbed the pack of beers and carried it over to the trash. She stomped on the foot pedal to open the lid on the trash can and was about to mindlessly throw the six-pack into the garbage, when she looked down at the pile and caught a glimpse of a section of the unmistakable beer-can label below some balled-up paper towels. With a disbelieving shake of her head, Rebecca threw the rest of the beers into the trash can, yanked the bag out of the can and, when the lid didn't close fast enough, she slammed it down to shut it. Holding the bag tightly in her hand, she marched outside, went straight to the large blue trash can that was stored on one side of the house and, with more force than she really needed, pushed the lid open and slung the bag in. It landed with a thud at the bottom of the near-empty can. Winded from weariness and emotional upset, her shoulders slumped at the thought of the conversation that was coming with Shane, Rebecca slowly walked back to the porch. Inside of the house, she leaned back against the door and closed her eyes. It was a breach of a fragile trust that had been built between them; a breach of trust that involved her *son*. And, like it or not, she had to address it.

Perhaps she was avoiding the inevitable, or perhaps she was just too busy, but Rebecca didn't have an opportunity to have the "talk" with Shane until Caleb was well enough to return to school and she had caught up at work. On her way home from the hospital, she had thought to ask Shane to watch Caleb while she returned to work the next day, but after finding the beer, she had changed direction and scrambled to find a sitter. She had finally called Kelly, and her sister, who knew just about everyone in town, found her a couple of leads. She had to miss an additional day of work until she could interview and then hire an empty nester named Felicia, who had a kind, fleshy round face and the faint scent of butter and brown sugar on her clothing. To make up for the lost hours, she scheduled clients on Monday morning, during the time that she would normally spend with Shane.

At first, Shane didn't seem suspicious of the distance between them. But when she ran into him in the driveway when she was on her way to work and he on his way to the VA for an appointment, she could read on his face that he knew something was off between them. It was time—she had put it off long enough. As they parted ways, she agreed to meet him on the bench after the boys were in bed. For the rest of the day, her stomach felt acidy and off. She had lost her appetite and skipped lunch, which only made her stomach feel worse. The sick feeling in her stomach lasted into the evening and was still with her as she made her way down the back porch steps. Normally, she would have a smile on her face and her pulse would be elevated at the thought of being kissed by Shane on a night like this. Normally, she would walk quickly to him, not wanting to miss a minute of private time with him. Tonight, it took her double the time to reach him.

Shane, who had been strumming softly on his guitar, stopped playing, but held on to the guitar.

"I was wondering if you were going to make it out tonight."

"I would let you know if not." She sat down beside him, but not as close as she would normally sit.

His thumb picked at the strings on his guitar; he didn't move to kiss her or put his arm around her. This night was, just from the tense silence between them, different than any other night they had spent together. Their relationship, even in its infancy, had been easy. Comfortable. She could feel how stiffly Shane was holding his body away from her, how tightly he was holding the guitar in his hands. Rebecca looked off in the distance, trying to force the words she had been crafting, drafting, revising and rehearsing in her head for days out of her mouth.

"Shane, we need to talk."

Rebecca spun her head toward the man sitting next to her. While she had been trying to pry words loose, he filled in his own version of what he thought she might be thinking.

For the first time since she had arrived, their eyes met. His eyebrows raised slightly and he asked, "Right?"

"Right."

He carefully, stiffly set his guitar aside and then leaned forward, resting his hands on his thighs, his fingers forming a steeple that rested on his lips. He moved his fingers away from his lips for a second, just long enough to say, "Let me hear it."

There was a crack in her voice even after she cleared it. "I'm going to ask you a question."

"Shoot."

She glanced at his profile. "Did you drink the night you watched Carson?"

Shane tapped his fingers to his lips several times while he thought. She wondered if he was contemplating the risk of lying to her.

He rotated his shoulder a couple of times, but that was his only movement for several breaths. Finally, he said one word. "Yes."

That one word, plainly spoken, made her take in a sharp inhalation of breath. It wasn't that she hadn't expected his answer to be "yes"—yet it made her feel like micro bolts of lightning were exploding in different spots in her body. A chill shook her even though it had been an unusually warm night. It was different to think that you know something and quite another to have it confirmed, without emotion and without, in her opinion, regret.

"Carson was asleep. I was exhausted," he said, by way of explanation. "I couldn't get to sleep..."

His voice trailed off. Perhaps he realized that his explanation, said aloud, sounded hollow.

She pressed her hands together and squeezed them protectively between her knees. They didn't speak for a couple of very long minutes, until she said in a quiet, even voice, "I love you, Shane. But if I can't trust you with my sons, I can't trust you with my life."

Shane took a sharp breath in and she knew that he got the implied meaning behind her words.

"This is over?" It was a question, but it sounded more like a statement.

Rebecca stood up, her arms crossed in front of her, her shoulders rounded forward as she turned toward him.

"You have some pretty serious things in your life to work out, Shane." Her voice cracked again. A flood of emotion was about to break the dam, and for some reason, she didn't want him to see her cry. "I wish I could help you. I really do. But I can't. My sons have to come first."

Rebecca slipped the key into the door to the garage apartment. She turned the knob and pushed the door open, letting it swing wide as she looked inside. It looked so strange, so small, now that the furniture was gone. Taking a step inside, Rebecca couldn't stop remembering all of the moments she had spent with Shane in this space—the times they had laughed, the times they had talked and the times they had made love.

She opened the blinds, letting the daylight in. Shane had left the place spotless. He had the kitchen and bathrooms and carpets professionally cleaned. If she wanted to, she could rent it immediately. But Rebecca wasn't so sure that was the right move for her and the boys. She moved into the bedroom, standing in the center of the room in thought. He had moved while she was at work and the boys were in school to make it easier on all of them. Carson and Caleb were both upset that Shane was moving, but Carson was taking it the hardest.

Rebecca noticed something stuck between the carpet and the baseboard. She bent down and picked it up. It was one of Shane's guitar picks. She turned it over and over in her fingers before she tucked it into the front pocket of her pants. With one last look around, Rebecca left the bedroom, walked quickly through the living room and out the door. After she locked the door, she sat down on the bench that Shane had left behind.

"Well, Rebecca. You'd better figure out how to make lemonade out of these lemons."

Shane's face was hot and he couldn't figure it out. He was in that space between sleeping and waking, where his dreams mingled with reality and he felt as if he was floating. Somewhere in the distance, he could hear his mother calling his name, but when he tried to respond, he couldn't move his lips. And then the clouds parted and he was standing in front of a mirror, washing his arms with sandpaper and splashing salty water on his face...

"Shane."

Savannah shook her brother-in-law's booted foot. "Shane!"

With a groan, he pried his eyes open, only to wince and shut them against the bright sunlight. It took him a quick second to figure out that he was lying flat on his back, on his brother Liam's porch, and *that* was why his face was hot. Mystery solved. The salty water? Recon's tongue. The sandpaper washcloth? Top's tongue.

Shane gave Top, who was sitting regally on top of his stomach, an affectionate scratch under the chin while he blinked his eyes open. She was blurry, but Savannah was standing in her Sunday best, hands on hips, staring at him.

"Hey, Savannah."

When he started to sit up, Top jumped onto the porch. His head was pounding, his ears were ringing and he couldn't quite fit the pieces together about *how* he ended up on the porch when, last he could recall, he was in the living room, surrounded by all of his unpacked boxes.

"Hey, Shane."

He hugged Recon, who was patiently waiting beside him, panting from the heat.

"You need some water, boy?" he asked the dog. "Give me a minute and I'll get you some."

When he tried to stand up, the muscles in his legs seemed like they had turned to melting rubber and he fell backward. Savannah didn't curse all that often, but she cursed then. She called Recon and Top over to a nearby empty water bowl in the yard, turned on the spigot and filled it. Side by side, the cat and the dog lapped up the fresh water.

He pushed himself upright again. Savannah was back in position, hands on hips, her expression a mixture of disappointment, anger and indignation.

"I always defend you," she pointed out, punctuating her words with her hands.

"I know you do." His voice sounded as rough and scratchy as his throat felt.

"I *always* defend you," she repeated as if he hadn't heard her. "I always tell the family to give you a break, give you more time, be more understanding."

"I know." He dropped his pounding head into his hands.

Savannah had naturally red hair, but she didn't have a fiery temper to match. This was a first in their friendship. Shane forced himself to lift up his head and squint at his sister-in-law through sore, gritty eyes.

"You're pissed off at me."

She looked around as if she was talking to a crowd and said, "Get the man a prize, folks!"

"But," he implored, "would you *please* just lower your voice a little while you're chewing me out for *whatever* it is that I did?"

"Oh." She raised her voice a notch. "Is my voice hurting your head, Shane?"

"Savannah." He winced. "Tell me what I did and I'll try to fix it."

"Let me tell you something, Shane." She was speaking in her normal volume. "Rebecca is one of the nicest people I've met in a long time."

The moment she mentioned Rebecca's name, he was hit by a wave of nausea, not because of all of the booze he had dumped into an empty stomach, but because of the hole that losing her and her sons had left in his gut.

"I don't know what happened between the two of you because she won't tell me, but now she won't come to

151

the ranch for brunch. Now she's not going to let her sons spend time with me here over the summer."

"I didn't tell her she couldn't bring the boys here."

"No. She thinks it will be awkward for everyone. I told her that it would take a half a day on foot to walk from the main house to Liam's cabin, but she doesn't know how big the ranch is. All she knows is that *you're* here, and now she won't come."

"I'm sorry." He said the words and he meant them.

"She's my friend, Shane. I love her and I'm *keeping* her. I don't care how *awkward* it is for you."

"I love her, too." It was the first time he'd admitted it out loud to anyone other than Rebecca. More softly, he added, "I'm *in* love with her."

His confession seemed to wash the ire out of Savannah's body because she came over to sit next to him on the top step of the porch. Recon and Top trotted over and occupied the lower steps, and for a minute or two, all of them just sat there in silence, with the sound of the cows mooing in the distance and a flock of birds flying overhead.

"What are you going to do about it?" she finally asked in a volume much more appropriate for his throbbing head.

"About what? Rebecca?"

She nodded.

"I doubt there's anything I can do." He shook his head at the mountain of trust-building he would have to climb to reach the woman he loved.

"Shane." She sounded half surprised and half frustrated. "Seriously? If that's how you thought when you were deployed, how would you have accomplished anything?"

"That was different. I had my orders. I had a mission."

"Maybe," Savannah said after a moment, "winning Rebecca back should be your *new* mission."

"I wouldn't even know where to begin."

"You begin by throwing away the beer, Shane. You could begin by going to the VA and taking the help they offered for your PTSD."

When he didn't respond, she continued, "Look. You've been trying to treat it yourself, in your own way, for years, and it's not working. You have to know that."

Savannah reached for his hand as if she was afraid that he was going to leap off the porch and literally run away from the topic.

"I don't want to talk about it."

"I know you don't."

"I don't want to *talk* about it."

He'd been offered medications that specifically treated PTSD symptoms, as well as sessions with a counselor specializing in combat-related trauma. But he had refused the help. He didn't want to talk about it then, and he didn't want to talk about it now.

"You've shut us all out for years," she said, an emotional catch in her voice. "All of us. None of us know what happened to you, Shane, because you won't tell us."

He didn't respond.

"Rebecca loves you. I can see it in her face. And her boys love you, too."

"I love them."

"Then *do* something about it." Savannah gave his hand a little shake. "Get your act together. Go get the help you need. Get your life in order and win her back, if that's what you want. But if that's what you really want, you're going to have to start with sobering up and getting right with God. She's a mother, Shane. She can't be with a man who she has to step over on the way to church because he's passed out on the porch."

Chapter Twelve

"Savannah!" Rebecca's eyes lit up when her friend walked through the door. She rushed over to give Savannah a lengthy hug. "I'm so glad you could make it."

"Oh, Rebecca." Savannah looked around the room. "It all came together. It's so clean and modern and *bright*. It doesn't even look like the same place."

"It's been a lot of work," Rebecca said. "I hope it was the right decision."

Savannah reached out to touch her arm. "It was. And I am honored to be your very first client."

After Shane moved out, Rebecca had locked the door to the garage apartment and left it sitting empty for nearly a month while she juggled work, baseball practice and games, along with the new summer schedule. Without the extra rent money from Shane, and with the new bill for childcare for the boys, Rebecca was constantly under financial stress, so much so that she had to go the doctor to get medicine for acid reflux. It was that moment that made her realize that she needed to make a change. She needed to be brave. She needed to be bold. She needed to take a leap of faith and open her own business. Savannah was the one who had first pointed out that the garage apartment had all the bones for a salon. That was the beginning of a new phase of her life for Rebecca. She secured a small business loan and, to her surprise, Kelly came in as a silent investor. The infusion of cash from her sister allowed her to give notice at Baily's salon, reduce the number of hours she needed for childcare and spend her summer renovating the garage apartment to become her very own salon.

"Do you want the tour?" Rebecca smiled broadly. "It's a quick one."

The space had been redesigned to include a small changing room, space for two stations, two sinks, a cozy waiting area and a remodeled bathroom. There was also a small room in the rear part of salon for Carson and Caleb to do homework when she had late clients.

"It's perfect." Her friend gave her another excited hug before she headed into the changing room to put on a smock.

Rebecca couldn't stop smiling as she warmed-up the water at one of the sinks. Clip Art Salon was her dream come true. Turning the apartment into a salon had gone a long way to fill the vacuum that had been left by Shane.

Savannah emerged from the dressing room wearing a smock. Rebecca patted the chair. "Have a seat."

Her friend sat down in the new chair. "It's super comfortable."

"The place is small, so I tried to make everything lux." She smiled. "Massage?"

"Absolutely." Savannah took the controller for the massage feature on the chair.

Her friend closed her eyes while she washed and conditioned her long auburn hair. As was her custom, she didn't engage her client in conversation while she washed her hair—she liked to make this a time of relaxation for them. She massaged Savannah's scalp and neck before she wrapped her wet hair in a towel.

"Wow." Savannah stood up. "*That* was incredible."

Rebecca followed her friend over to the chair at her station. "I was voted best scalp massage two years in a row back in New Hampshire."

Standing behind the chair, Rebecca combed out the knots in Savannah's hair. "There are a lot of split ends back here."

"I know." Her friend wrinkled her brow with a nod. "I hate to even admit this, but I think I've only had my hair cut once since Amanda was born."

"New-mom syndrome." Rebecca held up the ends for her friend to see. "I think I should take about three inches off the bottom."

Another nod. "Do it. My hair's got to be on point for Saturday."

Rebecca had been volunteering with Savannah's foundation to organize the fall silent auction. Savannah had started the foundation as a way to honor her son, Samuel, who had accidentally drowned as a toddler. At first, the foundation was only focused on building awareness for common household dangers for accidental drownings, but the foundation had been such a success that Savannah expanded the purpose to provide financial assistance to families with mounting medical and therapy bills for children who had survived near-fatal drownings. It was a worthwhile cause and Rebecca felt proud to be associated with such an important foundation. But she was feeling a mix of emotions regarding the silent auction. Shane would be performing at the event and it would be the first time that Rebecca had seen him since he moved out. It had been months and she knew herself well enough to know that her feelings hadn't faded for the man. She missed him. She loved him. And she had a nagging sense of dread about coming face-to-face with him again.

"Thank you, Rebecca." Savannah beamed as she admired her shiny, thick, sleek hair. "It hasn't looked this good in a long time."

At the door, the friends hugged each other tightly. With her hands resting on the upper part of Rebecca's arms, Savannah had a concerned look in her bright green eyes when she asked, "Are you sure you're okay with seeing Shane on Saturday? I want you there, but I get it if you're not ready."

The sound of Shane's name spoken aloud, as it always did, made her stomach clench in the most uncomfortable way. Rebecca had to fight not to let the pain she felt in her body reflect in her eyes or her facial expression.

"Savannah." She hugged her friend again as a way to break the eye contact. "Please stop worrying about me. Saturday is about the foundation, it's about honoring your son, and wild horses couldn't keep me from attending."

Rebecca stared at her reflection in the bathroom mirror. She had gained weight, there was no doubt about it.

She smoothed her hand over her stomach, which was now more pooched than she would want. It was the day of the silent auction and she had been holed-up in her room for hours, preparing. Kelly had gone shopping with her when it became clear that she had grazed her way into a larger dress size. She had only cried once over Shane; it wasn't until she couldn't zip up her pants that it hit her that she had been trying to eat her feelings away. Kelly had an eye for fashion, so Rebecca trusted her when she selected a forest green wrap dress that made the best of her hourglass figure and hid some of the weight she had packed on. But she was sweating profusely and currently had a tissue stuck to her forehead in an attempt to soak up the perspiration. At this rate, she would have to reapply her makeup before she even left the house.

"Seriously?" She noticed that there was yet another sweat stain forming beneath her right armpit. Only her right armpit was sweating excessively, which was weird on its own. Frowning, Rebecca lifted her arm, turned on the hair dryer and pointed it at the stain to dry it. Once the stain faded, she took one last look at her reflection and shrugged.

"This is you," she reminded her reflection. "Pick yourself up—don't put yourself down."

Would she prefer that she hadn't put on weight? Yes. Would she have preferred for her self-esteem to be soaring when she saw Shane for the first time? Absolutely. But what really mattered was the success of the silent auction, and if she focused on that, perhaps her own self-consciousness would fade into the background. She slipped into a pair of pumps, walked into a spray of perfume and received two thumbs-up on her appearance from each of her boys on her way out the door. On the way to the Baxter Hotel in downtown Bozeman, her nerves were making speed and she had to keep on reminding herself to slow down and stop gripping the steering wheel so tightly that her fingers ached. A moment she had been both anticipating and dreading was only five minutes away. Shane Brand was only five minutes away.

When he agreed to sing at the Sammy Smiles event, Shane knew that there was a good chance that he would get to finally see Rebecca. It wasn't the reason he agreed—he was happy to donate his voice to the cause—but it would be a mighty big bonus. Shane wanted a chance—just a chance—to show Rebecca how much he'd worked to excise his demons. At the very least, she would be seeing him sober, completely sober, for the first time since the day they met. Shane didn't believe that Rebecca was going to see him sober, swoon and fall into his arms like a twentysomething coed without missing a beat. Rebecca was a woman, a self-possessed, professional woman with responsibilities. But he was hopeful that, at least from the occasional morsel of information from Savannah, Rebecca still cared for him. That could be a start, a place from which they could begin again.

While he played, he watched the double sets of doors that led into the main ballroom at the Baxter. As the crowd grew, filling in the empty spaces in front of the stage, Shane fought to concentrate on the music instead of the sinking feeling in his gut that Rebecca wouldn't show because of him. Before, he would have buried his feelings with a beer. Lately, he had been learning how to channel his discomfort into his music, because he was more anxious without a couple of beers in him and performing in front of a crowd sober still felt odd; he was accustomed to blurry faces in the audience.

"Thank you," he said into the microphone after he finished a song. "I'd like to dedicate this next song to one of the people I admire the most in my life—my sister-in-law Savannah."

Savannah was standing, surrounded by his family—all of his brothers were in attendance, as well as his sister-in-law Kate and his parents. She turned in surprise, her sweet green eyes wide. She blew him a kiss and he winked at her. Halfway through the song, Shane closed his eyes, and when he opened them again, he saw Rebecca standing just inside one of the doorways. When their eyes met, and held for only a second, Shane got distracted and played the wrong chord.

He tracked her with his eyes as she made her way over to Savannah and his family. In his mind, Rebecca stood out in the crowd, wearing a forest green dress cinched at her waist. Her hair was longer now, and it fell in soft ringlets around her shoulders, framing her sweet face in the most charming way. It took a lot of control not to put down the guitar and go to her. How many times had he imagined her face at night, when he was alone in his bed? How many times had he wanted to pick up the phone because he ached to hear her voice? Shane forced himself to focus on the music, to move his eyes across the crowd instead of indulging in his desire to keep his eyes on Rebecca. There were five more songs in his set and then he would have his chance to go to her. The thought of being near her again, close enough to touch, close enough to look into those pretty eyes, made it difficult for him to keep his hands from shaking as he held his guitar.

Shane knew he rushed the last two songs. He thanked the large crowd applauding him, set his guitar in a nearby stand and hopped off the stage. So many people wanted to stop him to talk, to praise him, to tell him how much his music meant to them. And he appreciated them. He really did. None of them could know that they were only holding him up from his mission to find Rebecca; none of them could know that he only had Rebecca in his mind.

Shane moved through the perfunctory greeting and small talk with his family as quickly as he could without being rude. Then he leaned down and whispered a question in Savannah's ear.

"Where is she?"

Rebecca walked slowly through the smaller ballroom at the Baxter, where they had set up the silent auction. So many community members had donated service packages, handcrafted furniture, antiques and artwork. To see all of the items assembled in one place was impressive. Rebecca lingered on each item, trying to get her racing pulse under control, glad for the distraction of the auction. When she walked into the main ballroom and saw Shane on stage, her anxiety shot up like a Yellowstone Park geyser. It felt like she had a swarm of bees racing through her veins; her hands were shaking and her heart was racing as if she was a teenage girl confronted with a high school crush. She had almost left, not at all sure she was ready to see Shane again in that moment, but Savannah spotted her and waved her over to meet the rest of the Brand family. There were so many Brands that Rebecca couldn't keep them all straight. And the brothers, Bruce, Liam, Colton and Gabe, seemed like Shane Rorschach tests. If she squinted her eyes, they all had Shane's face, minus the beard.

"I want to see what's in the auction room," she had said as she excused herself from Shane's kin. The last thing she wanted was to have a reunion with Shane in front of his family. It was the perfect excuse because it wasn't a lie. She really did want to see the auction items.

Out of all of the auction items, a painting of a white chapel on a hill was the item that held her attention the longest. After she took a turn around the entire room, she wove her way through the crowd, back to the painting. She felt someone join her, and perhaps it was a lucky guess, or perhaps her awareness was tuned to him, but she knew it was Shane before he spoke.

"My great-great-grandfather built that chapel." He was standing beside her, but not too close, with his hands hidden in the front pockets of his slacks.

"Are you serious?"

"That's Bent Tree Ranch, where my father grew up," Shane told her. "Right outside Helena."

Rebecca was enchanted by that little chapel; before Shane had joined her, she was trying to imagine what it might be like to be married in that chapel on the hill.

"Is that chapel still there?"

"As far as I know." He leaned forward to examine the painting more closely. "It looks like this is one of my cousin's recent paintings."

For the first time since he had arrived, she looked at him. "Your cousin?"

"Jordan." This was said with a nod.

"He? She?"

"She."

Rebecca looked back at the chapel. "She's very talented. I feel like I could just walk right into the painting and go inside the chapel."

After a moment of silence between them, she added. "I would love to go there."

"I've never actually seen it myself."

They naturally began to walk around the room, stopping at certain items and passing other items by. It was as if they hadn't missed a day—the easiness between them present from the very beginning hadn't diminished. It made Rebecca wonder why she had spent one second of a day sweating through her clinical strength deodorant, worrying about seeing Shane again. Her nerves had gotten the better of her and now it all seemed so silly.

"The ranch isn't in your family anymore?"

"No. It's still in the family. My uncle inherited Bent Tree."

Rebecca sneaked a sideways glance at Shane—he was wearing a charcoal-gray suit with a steel-gray button-down shirt. His long hair was slicked back into a pony-tail, and she could see that he had made some unsuccessful attempt to trim his unruly beard. She'd never seen him in anything other than jeans and old T-shirts. This dapper side of Shane appealed to her. If only he would lose that terrible beard.

"There was a dispute over my grandfather's will, and my dad hasn't spoken to his brother since I was a kid."

"That's sad."

Shane nodded his agreement as he checked his phone

for the time. "I've got to head back for my next set. Walk with me?"

On their short journey back to the main ballroom, at least thirty people stopped Shane to talk about his music. Several people asked him specific questions about a trip to Nashville. When they managed to come out of the other side of the gauntlet, Rebecca asked, "Nashville?"

Inside, it bothered her that so many people seemed to know about Shane's life and she didn't. It was irrational, sure. But that was how she felt, regardless of rationality.

"I had a meeting with a record label," he told her. "Someone posted a video of me on YouTube, and the next thing I know, I've got a guy from a label approaching me after a show."

"Shane! That's wonderful." Not thinking, she rested her hand on his arm like she had a hundred times before.

Shane looked down at her hand on his arm with a strange, unreadable expression on his face. Rebecca drew her hand away, but Shane caught it and held it in his. He ran his thumb over the top of her hand and then, instead of letting go, he locked his hand with hers and led her through another throng of people to a less crowded area in the lobby.

"Your set." She glanced over her shoulder, knowing that they were heading in the wrong direction.

"It'll wait for just a minute." He stopped beside one of the tall ornate columns in the lobby, a place where people were walking past but not lingering.

He turned to face her, his hands back in his pockets. "This is important."

In the brighter lights of the lobby, Rebecca saw how clear Shane's striking blue eyes were now. She knew from passing comments that Savannah had made to friends at church that Shane had stopped drinking, and it showed. His face was leaner and tan, when his skin used to have a reddish, puffy quality; he looked so much healthier now.

Concerned that he was about to start a conversation that they couldn't finish in such a public place, Rebecca tried, once again, to point out that he was late for his next set. But he wouldn't be deterred.

"I promised myself, if I saw you today, that I wouldn't do this." He gave a small self-recriminating shake of his head. "But I don't know when I'll get another chance."

Shane paused, his eyes on her face.

"I'm sorry, Rebecca," he said quietly, plainly.

"I know you are, Shane." Tears that she hadn't felt like crying for months rose to the surface, and she had to steel herself to stop them from falling onto her lashes.

"I let you down." She saw Shane swallow several times, as if he shared her difficulty with keeping his emotions in check. "I let your sons down."

Her eyes slipped away from his for a moment. Carson and Caleb had taken it hard when they found out that Shane had moved out of the garage apartment. But when Carson found out that Shane had resigned as his coach before the season had even begun, her eldest son's hurt manifested into anger. It had never occurred to her that Shane would leave his coaching position, and she knew that Carson believed, no matter how many times she tried to convince him otherwise, that she had done something to get him to quit. Carson had come home from practice, slammed the front door, threw his glove on the couch and scowled at her for the rest of the night.

It was a shock to Rebecca; he hadn't reacted that dramatically when he found out about the divorce.

"I miss you, Rebecca. I miss our friendship." She heard a catch in his voice. "I miss your boys."

"We miss you." Those words were so easy for her to say because they were so true. Shane's absence had left a hole in all of their lives.

He paused, as if he were struggling to find the words he wanted to say next.

"Shane." She reached out and touched his arm. She instinctively wanted to comfort him. She could see the pain, the regret in his eyes. "We should talk about this later."

"You're right," he acknowledged after a split second. "I need to get back. I just needed to tell you that I'm sorry, that things are different for me now and if you could find it in your heart to forgive me, I'd really like another chance to be your friend."

Chapter Thirteen

Rebecca hadn't seen Shane in months and then, seemingly overnight, following the silent auction, he seemed to be popping up in her life in the most unexpected places, including performing at her church on Sunday. Their pastor announced that there was going to be a special guest playing a selection of spiritual songs, and one of the last names on the list of people Rebecca would have guessed would be Shane's. Whenever she had asked him to join her for service, he'd always said the same thing: *That's not the right place for a man like me.*" And then, unexpectedly, Shane, looking dapper, tall and trim in a navy blue suit, walked out onto the stage at the front of the church with his guitar.

"Mom." Carson's expression, which normally looked as if he were being tortured by the service, brightened. "It's Shane."

"Mom," Caleb said too loudly. "Shane's up there."

"I see." Rebecca put a quieting hand on her son's leg. "Keep your voices down, please."

"Shane is the guest?" she then whispered to Savannah. "Did you know?"

She gave a small shake of her head. "I knew he was asked, but I didn't know he'd accepted."

Shane stood behind the microphone, comfortable in his own skin on stage in a way that he didn't seem to be when he wasn't in front of an audience with a guitar in his hands.

Amplified by the microphone, the familiar timber of Shane's baritone voice filled the soaring ceilings of the grand old church.

"Thank you for inviting me," he said to the pastor. Then to the congregation, he said, "It's an honor to be with all of you today."

The sudden appearance of the man she still loved made her have an immediate and uncomfortable fight-or-flight response—her palms started to sweat, her body felt like it was shaking from the inside out, her skin felt hot on her neck and cheeks, and her heart started to beat harder and faster. She felt an odd mixture of happiness, nervousness and sheer curiosity. Never once, in all of the times he had given her a private concert on their bench, had he ever played a spiritual song. She hadn't known that Shane had this in him.

When Shane sang the first note of the song "I Can Only Imagine," her mind stopped whirling as her ears listened. She forgot her nerves and her discomfort and, like everyone else in the church, her eyes and her attention were fully on Shane, his voice, the words of the song and the sound of the guitar. Later, when she reflected back on the moment, she couldn't pinpoint what had touched her—it could have been a single lyric or the open honesty in his voice—but somewhere during the first song, Rebecca had begun to cry and, once the tears started, she couldn't get them to stop.

"Mom. What's wrong?" Carson had asked her. "Are you okay?"

She had nodded, took his hand and held on to it, glad that her son didn't pull his hand away, even when she knew Carson believed he was *too old* to hold her hand anymore. Shane hadn't stayed for the rest of the service—he had sung his songs and then he was gone, leaving her wanting more. More of his music. More of his time. Shane had asked to come back into her life, into her sons' lives, and she had considered it, but Rebecca had decided after the divorce that she wasn't going to let men come in and out of their lives mindlessly. The boys still didn't know that she had been romantically involved with Shane, yet they had gotten hurt anyway. As far as Rebecca was concerned, Shane had to earn his way back into their lives. And as much as she missed him—and she did—she was gun-shy.

"I promised Jock and Lilly that I'd invite you to Sunday brunch again," Savannah said as they fell into the line of parishioners filing out of the church.

Rebecca had met Savannah's in-laws at the Sammy Smiles event and it had only taken a few minutes for her to hit it off with Shane's parents. Jock was rugged and gruff, with silver-white hair, deep-set blue eyes, Shane's eyes, and wrinkles carved into his tanned forehead, around his eyes and mouth. Like Shane, his father was rough on the outside but seemed to have a tender heart beneath all of that prickliness. Lilly, Shane's stepmother, was a sweet soul, welcoming and gracious.

"Why don't you come?"

Savannah was the only family member, to Rebecca's knowledge, who knew about the nature of her past relationship with Shane. They had discussed the relationship once, and then they focused on other things. Their friendship had never been about Shane, and neither of them wanted to damage the closeness they had built between them.

"I want to go see the horses," Caleb, who had hung back with her instead of bolting out the door with Carson, chimed in. "I was supposed to be going riding."

Caleb had *not* forgotten that he had been invited to go riding at Sugar Creek Ranch over the summer and she hadn't let him go once things fell apart with Shane.

"There are plenty of horses to meet," Savannah told Caleb, shifting Amanda in her arms.

Carson was waiting at the car for them; Savannah was parked nearby. If Rebecca said yes to brunch, she knew that she was saying yes to more than a meal. She had overheard one of Shane's brothers mention that Shane had started to attend those brunches; if she agreed to go, she would be opening the door wider for Shane to walk through and back into their lives. It was a risk, but the Shane she had seen in church and around town lately was a Shane she was interested in getting to know.

"What do you think, Carson? Do you want to go to eat lunch at the ranch?"

"Yeah," her son said with a noncommittal shrug. "I think that'd be cool."

* * *

Shane ran through a path in the woods, pushing his body to go faster. He flew over a familiar creek like he was clearing a hurdle on a track, prepared to hit softer ground on the other side. He landed easily, got his footing and then kept right on running; he knew this path like he knew his own hand. This was the same path he would run when he was in high school. Ignoring the burning in his thighs and his calves and his lungs, Shane wove his way around overgrown trees, ducking his head to miss branches, and bolted forward into a clearing. Winded and sweaty, he checked his watch and saw that he had just broken his own record from when he was in his teens. Laughing, he raised his arms over his head and paraded around like Rocky Balboa after he reached the top of the steps of city hall. His body was starting to snap back after years of abuse, and now that he was reclaiming his health, mental and physical, it had become a passion once again.

Wiping the sweat off his face with the bottom of his T-shirt, he climbed the grassy sweeping hill that led up to the back door of the main house at his family's ranch. He pulled the earbuds out of his ears and let them dangle around his neck as he opened the door. He was usually the last to arrive at Sunday brunch—most of the time, he slid into an empty chair after the serving plates had been passed around once. But today didn't seem to be usual. His family was gathered just outside the dining room, talking animatedly and laughing.

"Shane!"

Caleb suddenly appeared, squeezing his way through the bodies gathered in the foyer.

"Hey, buddy." Shane gave the boy a hug.

Carson broke free of the group to greet him and that was when he saw Rebecca, still dressed in her Sunday clothes, standing next to Savannah. Their eyes met, and the moment he saw her, standing in the main house, his family home, he smiled. He knew that the invitation had been extended to Rebecca for a while now; he had hoped to see her there, but every Sunday, he was disappointed. When she smiled back at him shyly, it felt like all was right in his world again. How he had missed that woman's smile.

Carson didn't hug him; they shook hands instead. Both of the boys had gone through a growth spurt and Carson was lankier than ever.

"You missed all of my games," Carson said with his mother's bluntness.

His stomach muscles clenched like he had just been punched in the gut. "I know I did, Carson. I'm sorry. I was...sick."

"Mom told me." Carson nodded, unsmiling. "Are you better?"

Shane replied honestly, "I'm getting there."

After a second of thought, Carson switched the subject. "We're going riding later."

"Everyone." Lilly's voice rose above the din, interrupting his conversation with Rebecca's eldest son. "Brunch is served."

If he had known he was going to see Rebecca at brunch, he wouldn't have run there. He would have taken a shower, gotten cleaned up. Now he smelled like he hadn't taken a bath in a couple of days. And yet, he'd rather see her like this, disheveled and a bit stinky, than not see her at all.

"Hi, Rebecca." He caught up with her as she was heading into the formal dining room.

"Hi."

"I ran here." When he was around her, some of the most awkward things came flying out his mouth. But, he felt like he needed to explain his appearance to her.

Savannah squeezed into the space between them, linked her arm with Rebecca's and said, "No sense trying to get her to sit next to you, Shane. I've already got dibs."

The truth was, he didn't mind so much that Rebecca wasn't going to sit next to him, with a bucket of sweat drying on his clothes. Instead, he got to sit across the table from her and get his fill of her lovely face and pretty eyes. He'd originally started attending Sunday brunch to please Lilly and Savannah, but then he kept on attending in the hopes of seeing Rebecca. Now that she was here with her boys, the family felt complete to him.

"Hey!" He pointed at his brother Colton, feeling famished all of a sudden. "Don't hog all of those biscuits, brother."

After breakfast, as promised, Savannah's husband, and Shane's eldest brother, Bruce, took Carson and Caleb to one of the nearby barns to saddle up two of the calmest geldings in the herd. Brunch with the Brand family had been a blast for Rebecca. The fact that Shane was there with them, after she settled into the idea, only added to the fun. Shane's family was the exact opposite of her own family—they were loud and close-knit and in each other's business. They joked, they teased, they yelled occasionally, which always drew the disapproval of Lilly, and no one at the table, it seemed, wanted that. Her face hurt from the smiling and it was wonderful to see Caleb and Carson fit into the raucous clan as if they had always been there.

"Are you glad you came?" Shane asked her as he walked beside her on a rocky path toward the riding arena.

"Absolutely." She lifted her face up to the sun, glad for the warmth on her skin. They were going to be heading into fall and leaving behind short-sleeve weather soon.

"I was glad you came."

She looked at his profile. "Thank you."

They stopped together at the closed gate of the riding arena. Bruce had some ranch hands help him saddle three horses, find helmets for the boys, help them mount and then adjust their stirrups.

"Look at Caleb." She laughed. "He's in seventh heaven."

Caleb looked so small in a full-size Western saddle, but he was waving at her with his free hand and he was beaming.

"His horse is so big. He's the biggest one. Are you sure that'll be okay?" she asked Shane.

"Truck's the biggest, but he's the gentlest. That's why Bruce picked him," he explained. "Do you ride?"

"No," she said quickly with a shake of the head. "I mean, I can. But I don't want to."

He looked at her with a question on his face.

"I like horses. I like to feed them carrots and brush them, but I don't really like being *on* them. Too high up."

"You're afraid of heights?"

"Terrified."

"Note to self—no surprise hot-air balloon rides for Rebecca," Shane said as he watched the activity in the riding arena.

Bruce sat on his horse in the middle of the arena and watched the boys ride. He asked them to walk, trot, stop, turn the horses to the right and then to the left.

"You want to go on a trail ride?" he asked the boys once he seemed satisfied that they were strong enough riders to leave the safety of the arena.

"Yes," her sons exclaimed almost in unison.

"Mom? Can we go on a trail ride with Bruce?" Carson called out to her.

She nodded. "Just be careful."

Shane unlatched the gate and swung it open so Bruce and her boys could steer the horses through.

"How do I look?" Caleb asked her as he passed through the gate.

"Like a real cowboy." To Carson, she said, "Watch out for your brother."

"I will," Carson said, focusing on handling his horse.

"We'll be back in about an hour," Bruce told them. "I'm going to head toward Little Sugar Creek and then loop back."

Shane nodded as he shut the gate.

"Little Sugar Creek?" Rebecca asked.

"That's Gabe's homestead." He pointed to the south. "Pop carved out ten-acre homesteads for each one of his kids."

"Trying to keep you all together."

"Trying."

"That's nice." She stared after her boys, who became

smaller and smaller as they rode off into the distance. "You're lucky."

He met her gaze.

"To have such a big tight family. I always wanted that, but we don't always get what we want in life."

"I haven't always been so good to them," Shane admitted quietly, almost as if he were speaking aloud to himself. "But I'm working on it. I'm doing better."

Still watching her sons in the distance, she asked, "They'll be okay, right?"

"Besides Gabe, Bruce is the best horseman in the family. He'll watch out for Carson and Caleb like they're his own."

There were moments that she was with Shane and it felt as if time had never passed between them; and then there were other moments when her nerves kicked in and she felt afraid of getting too close. Having all of his family around for brunch and at the arena had given her a buffer; now they were alone for the first time since their break.

"Well," she said, "I suppose I should..."

He must have sensed that she was about to bolt back to the main house because he interjected before she could finish her sentence. "I want to show you something. Will you come with me?"

Shane ran up to the house and borrowed the keys to Colton's Jeep. It seemed to him that Rebecca was teetering on the edge of changing her mind about leaving with him, so he needed to get the keys, get her in the Jeep and get going before she could back out.

"Your chariot." He pointed to the black Jeep.

"You expect me to climb up there?"

Colton had jacked the Jeep up high to accommodate huge mud tires.

"I'll give you a boost."

"No." She held up her hand. "I can do it." Under her breath, she added, "Probably."

He stood back while she tried several times to get her leg up and still hold on to the frame of the Jeep, but she was too short to leverage herself up into the seat. Her cheeks were flushed and when she failed for a fourth time, and he was unable to hold back his laughter, she spun around and snapped at him. "Are you going to help me or not?"

Shane held up his hands in surrender. "You said you could do it."

"Well, obviously, I can't," she snapped but her lips were twitching and he could tell that she was holding back a laugh, too.

Still smiling, Shane put his hands on either side of her waist and lifted her up so she could get into the Jeep. Once she was in, she rolled her eyes.

"What is *wrong* with your brother?"

"He's still young and wild," Shane said as he climbed behind the wheel and put on his seat belt. "You up for an off-road adventure."

"Off-road?"

"I can take you out to the main road or I can take you on one of the ranch roads. It's a rougher ride, but it's a heck of a lot prettier."

"Ranch road." She had an excited glint in her eye that he liked to see.

"Buckle up, then." He cranked the engine. "I'm about to show you a good time."

Back when he was in high school, he would four-wheel all over the ranch for fun, but he'd never taken a girl with him. This was something he did with his friends or his brothers, so he couldn't be sure how Rebecca would react.

"Hold on." He glanced over at his passenger. "It's about to get bumpy."

From the corner of his eye, he saw Rebecca tuck her dress tightly under her thighs so the skirt wouldn't fly up and then, as he instructed, she held on to the exposed roll bar.

Shane came to a fork in the road and he took a sharp left, hit a bump and the Jeep lifted up off the ground. He heard Rebecca make a surprised noise and then she started laughing. The bumpier he made the ride and the higher he could get the Jeep to fly, the more she laughed. He was sorry to see his brother Liam's log cabin, his home for the last several months, come into view. He'd been having such a good time making Rebecca laugh that he didn't want the ride to come to an end.

"Doughnut?" he called out to her.

"No." She shook her head. "I'm full."

"No." He laughed and swirled his finger in a circle. "Doughnut."

"Oh! *That* kind of doughnut. Go for it."

Shane left the road and drove into a grassy spot, slammed on the brakes, and then he cranked the wheel hard and stepped on the gas, spinning the back of the Jeep around on a circle while Rebecca laughed and whooped beside him, her curly hair flying around her face in the most charming way.

They were still laughing when he pulled up in front of the cabin and shut off the engine.

"Well," she said, "*that* was a first."

Shane hopped down and nodded his head toward her. "Do you need help?"

"Nope." She unbuckled the belt, took her pumps off, swung her legs out and jumped down. "This I've got."

"I'm just going to let Recon and Top out."

Rebecca had her hands on her hips and a broad smile on her face. Her cheeks were rosy and her hair was wild from the wind. She looked prettier in that moment than he'd ever seen her look.

Shane opened the door and Recon bolted out, followed by Top, and they both raced right past him and went to say hello to Rebecca. She knelt down and hugged Recon around the neck and then turned her attention to Top, who was busy rubbing up against Rebecca's legs.

"Oh, my goodness, Top. You've gotten so big."

Top trilled loudly and then flopped down on the ground and turned upside down so her four paws were up in the air.

"They're still best friends?" she asked Shane.

"Inseparable." He nodded. "An unlikely pair."

She stood up, her pumps dangling from her fingertips. She caught him staring at her hair and she reached up with a small self-effacing smile. "It looks like I stuck my finger in a light socket, doesn't it?"

"A little," he said, "but it looks good on you."

"Oh, sure," she said, trying to smooth the curls down.

Shane started to walk and waved his hand so she would follow.

"This is Liam's house?"

He nodded.

"It's so private here," she said, looking around at the small homestead carved out of the woods.

"It's been good for me." Shane led her over to a metal storage barn and slid open the door.

"Wow." Rebecca stepped inside. "What is this?"

"What I wanted to show you." He flipped on a row of industrial lights that he had installed.

He had spent months converting one of the barns into an indoor obstacle course. He had tried to replicate, to some degree, the confidence courses he navigated during his time in the Army.

"You built all of this?"

He nodded, walking slowly beside her as she took in the sixteen different obstacles he had designed and hand built. Deciding to build this course had been his first step back to health; designing and executing the plan had been cathartic. Shane felt that he owed his life, in part, to the time he had spent in this barn.

"No wonder you're in such great shape," she said, her eyes still skating from one obstacle to the next. "You use all of these?"

"Instead of drinking." He needed to get this on the record with her. "I do this."

They reached the end of the barn and Rebecca turned around to look back at the distance they had walked before she looked at him. He wasn't mistaken, her eyes were watery with emotion as she said, "I'm so proud of you, Shane."

"Thank you, Rebecca. It means a lot coming from you." And for the first time in years, he was able to add, "I'm proud of myself, too."

Chapter Fourteen

The next Sunday, Shane played for the congregation, singing songs that had been requested by the parishioners and the pastor. Rebecca fully expected Shane to play and leave, as he had before. But this Sunday, he changed his routine. Instead of leaving, he entered from the back of the church, scooted past two church members and sat down next to Carson. Savannah leaned forward, smiled at Shane and winked at him before turning her attention back to the sermon. For the last round of hymns, Shane stood with them and sang. Every time she heard his voice, so clear and crisp, above the other voices, the hair stood up on her arms.

"Don't wait for me," Savannah said as the service ended. "I have to talk to Connie about the foundation. I'll see you at brunch?"

Rebecca nodded. All the boys had talked about for

the last week was going back to the ranch to go on another trail ride. She had enjoyed her time at the ranch, and although it was still awkward with Shane at times, things had smoothed out between them. Rebecca knew that he wanted to resume their friendship, and most likely their romantic relationship, as if nothing had happened. But he wasn't pushing her. He was just there, friendly, funny and *sober*, giving her a chance to adjust to a new normal between them.

"You stayed today." She said it as a statement, but it was more of a question.

He nodded.

"What did you think?"

"Not bad," he answered in a way that wasn't satisfying for her at all.

"*Not bad*—I'll never do it again? Or *not bad*—I'll do it again?"

He laughed and the sound sent a tingle of pleasure along her spine. After all of this time, Shane's effect on her body, as a woman, had never faded.

"Not bad, I'll probably do it again."

Satisfied, she smiled at him as she pointed to his scruffy beard. "Well, if you do become a regular, I think you need to do something about all that."

He rubbed his fingers over his beard. "You mean shave it off?"

Rebecca laughed at the expression on his face. "I wasn't suggesting that, really. But maybe it's time for a change?"

His beard had always been an issue between them; she was always after him to clean it up and he was always resisting the idea, preferring to keep it what he called "mountain-man chic."

Looking worried at the thought of losing his beard, Shane said, quite seriously, "It's like an old friend."

"I dare you to do it," she said, playfully, not expecting him to take the bait.

At her car, Shane said, "I'll tell you what. If you try my obstacle course with me today, I'll let you shave off my beard."

"Are you crazy?" she exclaimed. "I'm not climbing up on that Wall Hanger thing, or whatever you call it."

"You told me that your doctor said you need to start exercising."

It was true, she had told Shane about her physical last Sunday, which hadn't gone so well. She was overweight by a good twenty pounds, her bad cholesterol was high, her good cholesterol was low and her blood sugar was elevated. She had been so busy building her business that she had neglected her health and it was showing up in her blood work.

"She didn't say that I needed to put myself through boot camp," she retorted.

"Come on, Rebecca." Shane smiled at her charmingly. "You know you've wanted to shave this beard ever since you met me. Now's your chance. All you have to do is try."

"Now I'm sorry I even told you what the doctor said," she muttered, not one to back down from a challenge. He just stood there and smiled at her, undeterred by her grousing.

"All I have to do is try and you'll let me shave that terrible beard off your face?" she finally asked, beginning the negotiation of terms. "I don't actually have to complete all sixteen?"

She waved her hand at her boys, who were swinging on the swing sets in the church playground, to come over to the car so they could leave.

"Nope. You just have to try. *Actually* try." Shane emphasized the word *actually*, letting her know that she couldn't *pretend* to try and then give up. "Really," he added, "if you think about it, this deal is completely tilted in your favor."

"Do you need me to do anything else?" Carmen, her new intern, asked her.

"Nope." Rebecca shook her head. "I only have one more client today. I'll close up and I'll see you tomorrow."

Carmen grabbed her purse and headed to the door. It still amazed Rebecca that business was so good at Clip Art that she had enough clients to take on an intern.

"Have a good night," her intern said just before she closed the door.

"You, too."

Rebecca checked her phone. Her next client was due to arrive in a couple of minutes. She spent the few minutes of spare time straightening up her station. Every time she stretched out her arms or bent over, she winced in pain. She had taken Shane up on his challenge to try his obstacle course and she was still paying for it in sore muscles and stiff joints. Places hurt on her body that she hadn't even known existed. Satisfied with the neatness of her station, she headed to the restroom to wash her hands. She heard the bell on the front door of the salon chime.

"I'll be right there," she called out, wiping her hands off on the hand towel and hanging it on the towel rack.

She rounded the corner with a smile of greeting on her face, but her steps faltered when she saw Shane waiting for her in a space that he used to call home.

"Hi." She stopped by her station, her eyebrows drawn together in confusion.

"Hi." He returned the greeting, his eyes taking in the room. "I like what you've done with the place."

Shane knew that she had turned the garage apartment into a salon, but he'd never seen it. Rebecca picked at a rough fingernail to give her hands something to do. There was so much history between them in this space—this was where they had bonded as friends and where they had been lovers. Did he resent what she had done with this place after he moved out? Would she blame him if he did feel resentful?

"Thank you," she said. "It's a dream come true."

"You deserve it, Rebecca." He seemed to read the stiffness in her shoulders, because he added, "I'm happy for you."

She thanked him again, and her shoulders relaxed. "I'd give you the tour, but I have a client coming—" she checked her phone "—in just a couple of minutes."

"I'm your client."

Rebecca stared at him for a second and then checked the name Carmen had written in her appointment book.

"You're Brandy Smith?"

"In the flesh."

Per their deal, she had given the obstacle course her all. There were only two obstacles she refused to try because of her fear of heights. And yet, Shane hadn't mentioned one word about keeping his end of the deal.

"That's quite a beard you've grown, Brandy."

Shane ran his hand over his beard. "I just want to look like all the other girls."

Rebecca laughed. "I can definitely help you with that."

She gave Shane the ten-cent tour of the salon, rushing through the part of the tour that took them to the space where the bedroom had once been. It was impossible to be in that room with him and *not* remember what it felt like to have his hands on her body and his lips on her naked skin. What it felt like to have him inside of her...

Shane emerged from the changing room wearing a smock. Rebecca patted her chair for him to sit down. She grabbed her clippers and checked the blade and the setting.

"Are you sure about this?"

He looked at the clippers as though she was holding a very sharp knife. "A deal's a deal."

"I'm going to get the length off with these. Then I'll soften your beard with a hot towel, and *then* for the big finale, I'm going to give you an old-fashioned razor shave. Sound good?"

"Honestly? No." He frowned. "Are you sure you want to shave the whole thing off?"

"Oh, I'm sure." Rebecca turned on the razor with a smile. "I haven't been able to lift my arms above my head for a week, thanks to your *evil* obstacle course. This moment, right here, makes every second of pain I've felt *worth it*."

"You're staring at me again."

"I know." Rebecca was sitting beside Shane on their

bench, something they hadn't done since he moved away. "It's just that…"

He ran his hand over his clean-shaven jawline. "I'm devastatingly handsome?"

"Actually," she said, still staring at him. "Yes. You are."

Shane shifted his eyes to hers and smiled at her. Without the beard, he looked like a Calvin Klein model or a movie star. Sitting next to this new version of Shane made her stomach feel *fluttery*.

"I'm glad you approve."

"Well," she said, "I think any woman would."

"Maybe. But you're the one who matters to me."

Not knowing what to say in response, she said nothing at all, but the sweetness behind his words touched a soft spot in her heart for Shane. He had never wavered in his devotion to her, no matter how many women tried to capture his attention. She had seen the female reaction to Shane way back when she attended his show. Now that he looked like a soldier from a sexy army recruitment billboard, he was going to have a target on his back.

"I can feel the sun on my face." Shane rubbed his hand over his jawline again. "That's strange."

Then he turned those clear blue eyes to meet hers. "It feels strange to be sitting here on this bench with you again."

"I'm sorry."

He knew what she was apologizing for; she didn't have to explain. He shook his head, turning his shoulders toward her so he could look into her face.

"Don't you be sorry for anything, Rebecca," he told her. "You did the right thing breaking it off with me.

You did the right thing for Carson and Caleb, for yourself, and you did the right thing for me."

He reached for her hand, and she let him take it. The boys were with her sister and she felt as if she was back in her private bubble with the man she still loved.

"I was so screwed up, Rebecca." His voice trailed off as he added, "So screwed up." He shook his head as he continued in a stronger tone, "And when I lost you, when I lost the boys, it felt like I had lost everything worth having."

She squeezed his hand, hating that she had added to his emotional pain.

"But that was wrong," he continued. "*I* was wrong."

"You have so much to live for, Shane. So much music to share with the world."

He put his free hand over their clasped hands. "I haven't always been able to tell you what's been going on inside of me."

"No." She had always felt that there was an impenetrable wall between them, no matter how hard she tried to break through to him. Shane had always locked a big part of himself away from her.

He shifted his eyes away from her and stared off into the distance when he said, "I was diagnosed with PTSD several years ago."

It was a big admission from him, she knew that. But she wasn't surprised. Living with her dad's own undiagnosed PTSD, it was easy to spot some of the same issues in Shane.

"But I wasn't strong enough to..." He paused, regrouped and then restarted. "*Do* anything about it."

All she could think to do was sit quietly beside him and lend her support by listening.

He brought his eyes back to hers, eyes that were usually shuttered against any emotion but now had such raw pain in them that she felt it in her body.

"I've been doing the work," he explained. "Taking the medication, seeing a counselor at the VA. And I'm starting to feel…a little less like damaged goods."

"You've never been damaged goods, Shane."

If he heard her, he didn't acknowledge her words. "You might not believe this, but I never used to be a big drinker. I didn't really drink until I got out of the army."

"I believe you."

"I needed something to knock me out so I could sleep." His jaw hardened. "I needed something to make me forget."

"And now?"

He loosened his grip on her fingers, as if he suddenly realized that he was squeezing them too tightly.

"Now?" he repeated. "Now I don't try to forget."

They sat together in silence, their fingers intertwined, their shoulders touching. After a moment had passed, Rebecca asked softly, "Has it been hard not drinking?"

"No," he said without hesitation. "It wasn't hard to quit drinking. It wasn't hard to quit smoking cigarettes or getting high. It was hard to be without you, Rebecca. It was hard to be without Carson and Caleb. *That's* what was hard."

He didn't wait for her to respond. "You saved my life, Rebecca."

"No, I didn't. You did that, Shane."

"Ever since we've been apart, I've made it my mission to win you back. Wanting to be with you gave me the strength to finally face my demons. Wanting to be with you gave me the strength to get well.

"I had to do the work, Rebecca, but you were my inspiration."

Not having the words to respond, Rebecca wrapped her arms around Shane's waist and leaned her head on his shoulder. She felt him take in a sharp breath and then let it out slowly as he rested his chin on the top of her head.

"Are you ready, Rebecca?" he asked.

"For?"

"To give us another try?" Shane's voice wavered nervously. "Are you ready?"

Her heart beating so quickly in her chest, Rebecca lifted her head so she could look into Shane's handsome face. Was she ready? Until this moment, she hadn't been.

"What happened between us wasn't all your fault, Shane." She looked down at their hands. "I made mistakes, too."

He seemed to be holding his breath, waiting for her to finish.

"If I needed to keep what we were doing a secret, then I shouldn't have been doing it in the first place. That was just…wrong. And I'm sorry."

She met his steady but cautious gaze. "I love you, Shane. That's always been true."

The tension in his shoulders released and his jawline softened at her words.

"But?" he prodded when she couldn't seem to find her words.

"But," Rebecca continued, "Carson and Caleb have to be a part of my decision."

"Of course."

"Before I can say yes to you," she said slowly, measuring her words, "I need for *them* to say yes to you."

Chapter Fifteen

"I'm being ridiculous," Rebecca said to Savannah. "Why am I so nervous?"

She had her friend on speakerphone while she tried to curl her eyelashes with shaking hands. Every time she tried to get the eyelash curler near her lashes, her fingers would twitch from all the nervous energy she was feeling and she failed. With a frustrated noise, Rebecca threw the eyelash curler into her makeup bag.

"It's a first date," Savannah said, encouraging as always. "Everyone's nervous on a first date."

"Well, it's ridiculous," she grumbled.

Savannah laughed. "No, it's not. Quit being so hard on yourself. *I'm* nervous and I'm not the one going out on the date!"

"Oh, my goodness."

"What?"

"He's here." Rebecca picked up the phone from the counter. "I heard the doorbell."

Savannah made a smooch noise and said, "Send me a text when you get home. I can't wait to hear all about it."

Rebecca took one last look in the full-length mirror, pleased that she was back in the same size jeans she had been wearing when they first moved to Montana. Something had happened to her out on that obstacle course— she had gotten ticked off. The sore muscles, the stiff joints and back, and the fact that she could hardly catch her breath when she exerted herself made her so mad that she became determined to beat the course. When it had been good weather, the boys spent time with Bruce. When it was raining outside, they came with Shane and her to the obstacle course.

When she came out of the bedroom, Shane was sitting on the couch with Carson and Caleb and he had a game control in his hand. He glanced up at her and smiled.

"Ready?" she asked him.

"Just let him finish this one game," Carson said, not looking up from the screen. "He's about to go *down*."

"Yeah," Caleb parroted. "He's about to go down, Mom."

She exchanged a look and a smile with the babysitter, and then she sat down on a bar stool and waited for Carson and Shane to finish their game. This was one of the moments she had been so nervous about, the moment when Shane would come to officially pick her up, not as a friend, but as a man she was going to date. She had worried that her sons would act weird or treat Shane differently. Her fears were, as she could see now, completely unfounded. As it turned out, she was the only one who was acting weird.

Later, as they left the restaurant, they both laughed about how nervous they had been.

"At least I feel better knowing we were feeling the same thing," Rebecca said, holding Shane's hand.

It was liberating to hold his hand in public; it was liberating not to have to hide anything from her sons. She felt proud to be seen with Shane. Women liked to look at him, but what she loved the most about being with Shane was that he didn't look back at them. His focus, his attention, was on her and their date together. To have that kind of attention from such a handsome man was a natural high for Rebecca.

"I have to tell you," Shane admitted as they strolled hand in hand through downtown Bozeman. "When Carson opened the door, he looked every bit the man of the house and he scared me—just a little." He smiled down at her. "I won't admit that in mixed company."

She bumped her shoulder to his. "It'll be our little secret."

Out of her two boys, she had worried about Carson's reaction to her dating his "friend" Shane. But it was Caleb who had some confusion to work through. Her younger son felt that she should talk to their father and get his opinion. In a way, she understood. When they were married, Caleb saw them make decisions as a couple. That was one of the strengths of their marriage.

Mom doesn't have to ask Dad to go out on a date, Caleb. They're divorced, Carson had explained to his brother in plain language. *Dad can date who he wants and Mom can date who she wants. That's how it is now.*

"Then he challenged me to a game and that put me right at ease," Shane recounted.

"He's a pretty amazing kid," she agreed. "Both of them are, really."

"They have an amazing mother."

"If you keep on saying things like that, you're going to spoil me."

He brought her hand up to his lips. "It feels like I've been waiting a lifetime for a woman to spoil. I'm not going to stop now that I found you."

It didn't matter if they were talking, it only mattered that they were together. Neither of them were much into social media, other than for business, but they did take a selfie so that they could capture their first official date. They walked together, exploring shops and stopping to get a coffee. It was a night that neither of them wanted to end.

Rebecca sighed lightly when Shane pulled his truck into the driveway, shifted into Park and shut off the engine. He kept his hands on the steering wheel and stared straight ahead into the darkness of the night.

"This meant a lot to me," he told her. "No hiding. No lying. Just you and me. Together."

For Rebecca, this date was different than any date she'd ever had. It had been romantic, sweet and fun. It had been everything she'd ever dreamed of when she was a little girl about what it would be like to fall in love and have that love returned.

"Pop always said that if you were any type of man, you'd ask for the second date before the first one ended." He looked over at her, part of his face in the shadows. "So, I'm asking, Rebecca with the pretty eyes. Will you go out with me again?"

* * *

When they had first become romantically involved, things were so different. Shane wasn't sober and she wasn't being honest with her sons. Now they were free. What she had discovered very quickly was that Shane was a romantic—you wouldn't know it looking at him. Even with his clean-shaven face, he still carried himself with the rigidity of a military man. But he was, to her great delight, more romantic than she could have imagined. And certainly more romantic than she had ever experienced before. He would leave a single yellow rose, her favorite, in the door of Clip Art so it was there to greet her in the morning. He sent her the sweetest cards, all of which she kept in the nightstand by her bed. When she missed him at night, she would take out those cards and read them, over and over again, feeling so lucky to have a man love her as much as Shane loved her. How worried she had been when she divorced that she wouldn't ever fall in love, that she wouldn't ever be able to find a man who loved her sons the way that they deserved to be loved. And then came Shane.

"Where did you go just then?" Shane's voice brought her back to the present. The boys were back in school, and she had left her schedule open for the day because Shane wanted to take her on a picnic at the ranch.

Rebecca was lying on her back, eyes closed, listening to the wind moving the leaves overhead and the sound of the water moving over the rocks in a nearby stream. Shane had picked the perfect spot for a picnic, a clearing in the woods beneath a canopy of trees. It was fall, so they weren't bothered by bugs or the heat.

"I was thinking about us." She opened her eyes just a bit to look up into that handsome face of his.

He was leaning on his arm, lying on his side, watching her, closely, as he often did. It was as if he wanted to keep an eye on her so she didn't disappear.

"One of my favorite subjects." Shane leaned down and kissed her lightly on the lips.

"Hmm," she murmured sleepily. "What were you thinking about?"

"I was thinking about the Wall Hanger."

Rebecca's romantic bubble was burst, just like that. Her eyes popped open and she stared at Shane's profile. "Are you serious? We are on a romantic picnic and you're thinking about your obstacle course?"

He laughed at how upset she was at him. "I can walk and chew gum."

When he didn't continue, she prodded him, sitting up and pushing her curls out of her face. "So? What are your thoughts?"

"I was thinking that it's time for you to conquer it."

Now it was her turn to laugh. "You're relentless, Shane."

He lay back, his arm behind his head. "If you conquer the Wall Hanger, you can conquer the world, Rebecca. I sincerely believe that."

"Spoken like a true military man."

The Wall Hanger was her obstacle course nemesis—a basic nightmare for someone afraid of heights. It looked like an oversize jungle gym for adults, which had one side made for scaling the wall with a rope and then, at the top, a fun opportunity to dangle from a really high place, with only a rope to hold on to. The only way down was to either fall—no, thank you—or move, hand over hand, along the rope until she reached the end of the rope and could swing down. Shane had been pushing her to beat the Wall Hanger and she had been telling him, in every way she could say *no,* that it wasn't going to happen.

"Did you bring me out here to this beautiful place just to butter me up so you could convince me to get up on that torture device of yours?"

"I had something else in mind entirely."

She raised her eyebrow at him.

"I was thinking I could help you check the box on one of those bucket list items."

The man could always, *always,* make her blush. He still had a healthy sexual appetite, and ever since they had rekindled the physical part of the relationship, Shane liked to find time to sneak away with her so they could make love.

"Out here?" She looked around.

He nodded, hooking his finger through the belt loop of her jeans.

"There's nobody out here but you and me."

When she hesitated, he twisted his fingers in her shirt and tugged her forward. "Come here and love on me, Rebecca."

He guided her down gently—he was so gentle with her. Then he put his leg over hers and covered her body with his own. With his finger, he moved strands of hair off her forehead, staring down at her with such love, such admiration, that it almost brought her to tears.

"I love you, Rebecca," he said, his hand on her cheek. "I want you to know that I thank God for you every day. Every day."

She reached up and put her hand on his face. "I thank God for you."

He kissed her cheek and her neck and then kissed

her eyes closed. He lifted her arms above her head and threaded their fingers together. With a happy sigh, her fingers in his hair, her body ready to be loved, and with her eyes closed, Rebecca drifted away in her mind to a place where his touch, his breath, his lips and his murmured words were the only reality.

"Do you trust me?" Shane used his stern drill-sergeant voice when he asked that question.

"No!" Rebecca snapped at him.

She was frozen at the top of the Wall Hanger.

"Do you trust me?" he asked again.

"I don't know." She refused to look at him as she clung to the rope as if it were a lifeline.

"Do you trust me?"

"This is your fault, Shane. This. Is. All. Your. *Fault*. If I die an untimely death on this stupid thing, you will have to live with that for the rest of your life."

"You're not going to die."

"Quit debating with me, Brand, and get me down. I'm stuck up here like a cat in a tree."

Shane had to work to keep his lips from lifting into a smile. If Rebecca caught him with even so much as a hint of a smile on his face, she might hold a grudge for a good week or two.

He moved into her line of sight, forcing her to focus on his face.

Tempering his tone, he asked for the fourth time, "Do you trust me?"

"Yes!" she shouted at him, her knuckles white from the death grip she had on the rope. "Yes! I trust you. Now get me down. Get me down *now*."

"If you trust me, then you'll believe me when I tell you that you can get yourself down, Rebecca."

"Are you kidding me? That's your solution to this problem? Well, I don't like that solution. I want you to go and get a ladder so I can climb down off of this stupid thing."

Ignoring the ladder suggestion, he kept his voice steady, realizing that the drill-sergeant voice was the wrong choice.

"You've seen me do this a hundred times, Rebecca. You can do this."

"Be quiet."

"Just swing your legs down, hold on to the rope and let yourself fall. If you lose your grip on the rope, I promise I will catch you."

"I don't like you right now," Rebecca told him, but she did swing her legs down, which was progress.

It took her five long minutes, but Rebecca finally did what he had trained her to do—she secured her grip on the rope and then swung her body down. Just before she caught herself, she screamed. When she realized that her grip had held and that she was still alive, she told him to back off and let her do it. Hand over hand, one step at a time, he followed her as she made her way along the rope.

"You've got it. Just a couple of more inches." His heart was pounding watching her. Not because he was worried, but because he was proud. This was the only obstacle that had defeated Rebecca week after week. Today, she was kicking its butt.

Rebecca reached the end of the horizontal ladder, held on to the rope and then slid down slowly until her feet were on the ground. With a look of sheer amazement, she lifted up her arms over her head in celebration.

"Did you see that?" She hit him on the shoulder before she let him pull her into his arms for a celebratory hug. "I did it!"

He kissed her on the top of her head as he held her tight. "I knew you could, Rebecca. I never doubted you for a second."

"I'm still mad at you."

"I know you are." He laughed. "You wouldn't be you if you weren't."

After her triumph with the Wall Hanger, a triumph she never intended to have again, they rushed back to the cabin to take a shower and make love before they met the boys back at the main house. They didn't always have time to linger in bed, but Bruce planned on taking Carson and Caleb on an extended ride to a campsite for a cookout. So this was a rare moment when Rebecca could lie in Shane's arms, their naked bodies intertwined, the covers pulled up over her shoulders, and her hand resting lightly over his beating heart while he twisted her curls around his finger.

"Are you okay?" Rebecca tilted her head back to look at Shane's face. He was staring straight ahead, not really looking at anything in particular. He seemed so far away from her in that moment.

"You trusted me today," he said, quietly.

She waited for him to continue, feeling as if he had something important on his mind.

"And look what you accomplished."

His free hand was making a swirling pattern on her shoulder, around and around.

"I haven't trusted you," he continued.

Even though she was warm beneath the covers, a chill raced down her back and her hand stilled on Shane's chest. It wasn't just the words he had spoken—it was the distant, haunted sound in his voice that caught her attention.

"Shane...what's wrong?"

Suddenly, his skin felt clammy to the touch and she felt him shiver. The muscles in his neck tensed and his fingers closed over her shoulder.

"It was our platoon's last patrol before a three-day leave. One more day—just one more day, and we were all jacked up about it. Salvage—his last name was Salvo—but our drill sergeant at boot camp called him Salvage to get under his skin, you know, and it just stuck. Let me tell you—that guy had a sixth sense about trouble and we all got real superstitious about Salvage and his intuition. Out there—" Shane pointed his finger like he was pointing at something very specific "—you had to believe in something, so we believed in Salvage and his gut. That day, Salvage didn't feel a damn thing, so we were all feeling pretty good because Salvo's gut had never been wrong. But that day..." Shane paused for so long that she thought that maybe he wasn't going to finish. "That day was the worst day for his gut to get it wrong."

Rebecca held her breath and then let it out slowly. So many times, she had wanted to ask Shane about the burns on his back. So many times, she had stopped herself because something inside of her realized that this was his story to tell in his own time.

Once Shane started reliving the story, he didn't pause again. He spoke in a monotone, as if he was talking about a scene he saw in a movie, but there were tears streaming down his face as he spoke. Rebecca sat up and turned to face him so she could give him her full attention, holding on to his hand for support. He needed to get this out; he needed to trust her with his story, the way she had trusted him on the obstacle course. He told her about the ambush and the explosions. He told her about how the back of his uniform caught on fire when he pulled Salvage free of the wreckage. The blast had deafened him; he could see Salvage screaming in pain, but he couldn't hear him. His own back raw from the burns, Shane had dragged Salvage to safety just as a third explosion sent one of the vehicles up into the air.

"I couldn't save them." Shane looked at her, but he seemed to be staring through her. "I couldn't save anyone."

She reached over and wiped the tears from his face, fearing that she didn't have the right words—any words—that could comfort him.

"They all died." He said so it quietly, she had to strain to hear him. "I was platoon sergeant. They were my responsibility. And I got them all killed."

She wiped her own tears from her cheeks. It was no wonder Shane had been so sad; it had been no wonder he had difficulty sleeping.

"Salvage?" she asked with an emotional rasp in her voice.

When he looked at her this time, she knew that he was truly seeing her. "He died in my arms."

Shane looked away from her then and added, "I should have died that day, too."

"No."

He laughed but it was a hollow, humorless laugh.

"They gave me the Bronze Star for combat valor. Combat valor." He repeated the words. "I survived. They all died. I got a medal and a promotion."

Rebecca wrapped her arms around him, rested her face on his bare chest and hugged him as tightly as she could.

"I didn't want that medal," he told her. "I didn't deserve that medal."

She hugged him tighter still. "It wasn't your fault, Shane. You were so brave. You tried to save them. It wasn't your fault."

"I've still got a lot to work out with my counselor. That's just the long and short of it." He rested his chin on the top of her head and started to wrap her curls around his finger. "But I love you, Rebecca, and you deserved to know why…" He paused before he continued. "Why I am the way that I am."

"I love you," Rebecca told him. "Thank you for trusting me with your story."

Chapter Sixteen

"They are missing the first real snow of the season." Rebecca was standing in front of the window, watching the snow fall outside.

Shane leaned up on his elbow and rubbed his eyes to focus them. They had just spent Thanksgiving with his family, and the turkey must have gotten to him because, when they got back to the cabin, he fell asleep with Recon at his side and Top on his pillow when he had fully intended to make love to Rebecca.

"They'll be with us for Christmas," he reminded her gently.

Carson and Caleb were in California with their father for the Thanksgiving break and, even though he knew that Rebecca had enjoyed spending the holiday with his loud and boisterous family, she was missing her sons.

It was just past midnight, according to the clock on

his phone, and the snow, which had stopped earlier in the evening, had begun to fall again. Rebecca looked so beautiful in silhouette, the dark outline of her hourglass figure beneath the thin cotton of his white button-down shirt, her hair in loose long curls down her back. Drawn to her, Shane extracted himself from the pile of animals, shooing them out of the room and shutting the door. He walked up behind her and put his hands on her shoulders. In response, she put one hand over his to let him know that she was happy for his touch.

"Come back to bed," he whispered against her neck. "I'm lonely without you."

She turned in his arms and kissed him. Shane felt the curve of her thigh against his leg and the soft curve of her full breasts against his chest, and the thought of going back to sleep was pushed out of his mind, replaced by thoughts of making love to Rebecca. He ran his hands along her hips and up to her waist, pulling her body closer.

"Hmm." She made a pleasurable noise when he kissed his way up her neck and to her ear.

Playfully, she pushed him back toward the bed. Lately, Rebecca had been comfortable taking charge of their lovemaking, exploring her own power in the bedroom, and Shane didn't have any complaints. He liked a strong woman in the bedroom, and Rebecca had grown into that role.

Without hesitating, she stripped his boxers off and tossed them over her shoulder. She gestured for him to sit down on the edge of the bed. Whenever she bossed him around in the bedroom, as much of a turn on as it was, it made him want to grab her, throw her on the bed and take charge. But he resisted, knowing that his turn was coming.

Standing in front of him, Rebecca smiled at him and slowly unbuttoned the shirt of his that she was wearing. Instead of taking it off, she teased him by leaving it unbuttoned and open, showing the swell of her breasts. His eyes traveled down her curvaceous body; she had lost weight from their workouts—her muscles were more toned—but she was still voluptuous. She wanted to lose more weight, but he liked her just the way she was. She complained about her cellulite, but he never noticed it. What he noticed about Rebecca with the pretty eyes, from the very beginning, was her sweet, confident nature. Even when she wanted to lose weight, she loved herself. Even when she complained that her hair was too frizzy on a rainy day, she loved herself. And she put that love out into the world. Her philosophy was, "I like you until you prove me wrong," and he loved her for that.

"You are a thing of beauty, Rebecca."

She looked down at her body with a smile and ran her hand over her stomach. "Look how flat my stomach is now."

"You always look good to me."

"And my butt." How pleased she was with her own body now made him smile. "Have you really gotten a good look at it lately? It wasn't this tight when I was twenty."

"Now…" Over the material of the shirt, Rebecca cupped her breasts with her hands and pushed them upward. "If only exercise could stop these from heading south, that would be…"

Shane latched his fingers around her wrist and tugged her to him. He pushed his shirt down off her shoulders, exposed her breasts and trapped her arms, still in the sleeves, next to her body. He wrapped his lips around one of her puckered nipples and suckled it until he heard her make that sexy little noise that let him know that he had her full attention. He stripped the shirt off her body so he could run his hands over the soft skin of her hips and her thighs and her stomach.

"One day—" he replaced his hand on her belly with a kiss "—I'm going to put a baby right here."

In response to his promise, Rebecca put her hands on either side of his face and kissed him on the lips. "One day, I will have your baby."

Rebecca kissed his neck, his chest, his stomach and continued down his body until she was kneeling in front of him. And then her mouth was on him, so warm and wet. Shane threaded his fingers through her silky hair, closed his eyes and let her spoil him. Rebecca had become a student of his body, had studied him, learned what he liked, and it didn't take her long to become an expert on driving him crazy.

"Rebecca." He had to grit his teeth to keep from losing himself. "I keep them in the drawer."

A few minutes more and he wouldn't have been able to hold back. Rebecca got a condom out of the drawer, ripped open the package and handed it to him. He put it on as quickly as he could and then opened his arms for her. Rebecca stepped into his open arms and wrapped her own arms and legs around his body as she sunk down onto his lap. His moan mingled with hers; their bodies felt like one body, swaying and moving in a familiar rhythm that only they knew. He gripped her hips with his hands, burying his face in her neck and breathing in the scent of her skin. Rebecca made a little noise, her arms tightened around him and she pushed down harder, taking him deeper, and moved her hips more urgently.

"Yes, baby."

Her body tightened around him, she shuddered in his arms and then, only then, when he knew he had pleasured her, he stopped holding back and sunk deeper inside of the woman he loved and joined her in that pleasure.

"Tell me about Christmas at Sugar Creek." Rebecca was lying on her back so Top could sit on her stomach in a breadbox pose. Recon was at their feet on the bed and Shane was propped up on a couple of pillows. Since Caleb and Carson were in California with their father, she was spending the week with Shane at the cabin. They had become a close-knit little family of four, with Recon and Top vying for valuable real estate at bedtime.

In the aftermath of their lovemaking, instead of feeling tired, they both were wide-awake while giant flakes of snow floated down from the starless night sky.

"Man." Shane smiled at the question. "I do love the way we Brands do Christmas."

"Any family traditions?"

"Nothing but." He laughed. "Starting with going out in the snow to find the perfect fir tree to chop down."

"The boys are going to love that."

"We always decorate the tree on Christmas Eve and hand out stockings. Pop makes the eggnog—that's his contribution—and it's always spiked, so I'll be abstaining from that this year. We Christmas carol in town every year, take the sleds out on the hills around the ranch, bake cookies and decorate them, snowman building in the front yard, ice-skating on the pond, with hot chocolate, sleigh rides around the ranch…"

"Sleigh rides?" she interjected.

"Every year."

Rebecca looked over at him. "An actual sleigh?"

"My grandfather restored them as a hobby and, in his honor, we take it out every Christmas," he told her. "We have so much food—everything homemade."

"It sounds like a Norman Rockwell painting," she mused.

"It's my favorite time of year at the ranch." He reached out to take her hand. "And this year, I get to share it with you and your boys. I can't think of anything better."

Christmas at Sugar Creek Ranch was, indeed, a wondrous affair. The family had events planned during the weeks between Thanksgiving and Christmas, and Rebecca and her sons had been invited to them all. When she had first moved to Bozeman, she had worried that, with only her sister Kelly in Montana, her boys wouldn't have a sense of family. The Brand family had welcomed them, with an open door and open arms, into their world. And what a wonderful world it was for Carson and Caleb. Shane had told her about the activities at the ranch, but to experience it firsthand was an entirely different matter. The boys ice-skated on a Sugar Creek pond and built a giant snowman in the front yard of the main house. They had picked out a Christmas tree, not in a parking lot, but in the woods, and they had helped Shane and Bruce chop it down. She had lost count of how many rides in the sleigh Shane had given them.

But, the most magical part of the holiday was Christmas morning. Ever since her sons were born, Rebecca had wanted to give them an extravagant Christmas, with packages piled so high that they covered the bottom of the tree. Their Christmases had always been lovely and meaningful, but they had been humble. She had saved all year to buy her sons a couple of big presents and then filled in the space beneath the tree with smaller gifts. The Brands were a family of means and they had not excluded Carson and Caleb from the holiday bounty. There were so many presents beneath the tree for her sons that Rebecca found it difficult to hold back tears of happiness as she watched them rip open the presents, throwing the paper and the bows in the air and jumping up and down when they found tablets and video games inside. Bruce and Savannah bought them both Western saddles and Shane outfitted them with cowboy hats and boots and everything they would need to be authentic Montana boys. It was amazing and overwhelming. For her, it was the best Christmas she had ever had. And not just because of the gifts for Carson and Caleb—it was because they were part of a big loving family.

"We've overwhelmed you, haven't we?" Shane came up behind her.

"A little," she admitted with a smile. "But only in the best of ways."

Christmas was a formal affair at Sugar Creek Ranch,

and Shane looked so dapper in a black suit with a sprig of mistletoe pinned to his lapel. He put his hands on her shoulders and they stood together in front of the fire, quietly staring at the flames.

"Do you like your gift?" he asked.

"Oh, Shane." She turned around so she could look up into his face. "I can't believe you bought that painting for me."

The night of the silent auction, they had reunited in front of a Jordan Brand painting of a white chapel on a hill. It was one of the most beautiful paintings, to her mind, that she had ever seen. She wanted to walk into the painting and go inside that chapel. She had wanted so badly to bid on that painting, but with starting a new business and her sons to consider, she had let the painting go. Shane bought that painting for her and had given it to her for Christmas.

"It's the nicest gift anyone has ever given to me." She put her hand on his sleeve. "I love it."

"I love you, Rebecca."

"And I love you."

There were at least thirty Brands milling around the house, laughing and talking and celebrating the holiday. Most of the adults were loitering around the kitchen as dinner was about to be served, while many of the kids, including Carson and Caleb, were playing video games on a gigantic TV screen in Jock's den. The Christmas tree room had been abandoned; Rebecca had retreated to the space to catch her breath. It didn't surprise her that Shane had come to find her; he had been very attentive to her the entire day. His concern for her—his concern for her sons—only made Rebecca love him more.

Shane cocked a half smile at her while he unpinned the sprig of mistletoe from his lapel and held it over her head.

"Merry Christmas, Rebecca Adams."

She placed her hands on the lapels of his jacket, lifted up on her tippy toes and kissed him lightly on the lips.

"Merry Christmas, Mr. Brand."

In front of the fire, with all of the voices and nervous energy and loud laughter fueled by Jock's heavily spiked eggnog, Rebecca and Shane held each other tightly, taking a small private moment just for the two of them.

He stepped back from her, just enough to see her face, and he held her hands loosely in his. Shane was looking at her so intently, so seriously.

"What?" she asked him with a nervous laugh.

"There's something that I want to ask you, and now that the moment is here, I'm losing my nerve."

"You?" She shook her head. "Losing your nerve? Not possible."

"Oh," he disagreed, "it's possible."

She looked at his face intently, waiting for his next words. There was a fine sheen of perspiration on his forehead.

"Shane, you're scaring me. What's going on?"

"If I asked you to marry me, Rebecca, what would you say?"

Rebecca wasn't sure what she had expected for Shane to ask, but marriage hadn't made the list of the top ten. Of course they had discussed a future, marriage and children. But she didn't think that marriage had been on his mind in the here and now.

"I would say," she said, "that I love you and I have thought about marrying you many times."

She paused to consider her next words. "But it's not just me. So I would have to know that Carson and Caleb would be okay in this."

Shane had slipped his hands into his front pockets; he had an odd expression on his face as if he was steeling himself.

"What if Carson and Caleb liked the idea? What would you say then?"

She didn't like how he was standing, so stiffly, with his hands in his pockets. Rebecca slipped her hands through his arms and hugged him.

"Then I would say yes, Shane. Yes, to being your wife. Yes, to spending my life with you. Yes, to another child. I would say yes."

Rebecca stepped back and tugged his hands out of his pockets and held on to them. "Does that answer your question?"

She would have thought he would be smiling after all of those yeses.

"Are you sure about that?"

Rebecca frowned at him playfully, wanting to lighten his serious mood. "Now you're just fishing for another yes, and I don't think I'm going to give you one."

"I'm sorry to hear that," Shane said, and there was a new twinkle in his eyes and he whistled loudly, which was a strange thing for him to do in the middle of a rather important discussion about the future direction of their relationship.

Carson and Caleb appeared around the corner—she had thought that they were both on the other side of the house, playing their new video games. Her sons looked so handsome in their suits. Not only was she surprised to see them, but she was surprised to see that they still had on their jackets and ties.

"I thought you were playing your new game." She gave each of her sons a hug and straightened their hair, even though Carson ducked after a second of her fussing over his hair.

"We were," Caleb told her, standing on one side of Shane.

"They came to help me for a minute." Shane put one arm around Caleb's shoulder and the other arm around Carson's shoulder.

The three of her favorite men stood in a row across from her, and while Carson and Shane were pretty good at keeping a poker face, Caleb looked like he was about to burst.

"Why do I have a feeling that you guys know something I don't know?" She titled her head to the side and looked specifically at Caleb to see if he would crack.

"Because we do." Caleb grinned at her, looking like a jack-o-lantern because he had recently lost one of his front teeth.

"Should we give it to her?" Shane asked Carson and Caleb, his arms still around her sons' shoulders.

Carson reached into his front pocket, fished around for a second and then pulled out a small box. Rebecca stared at the box, and a burst of adrenaline shot through her body, making her feel prickly and hot and dizzy. She reached out for the mantel to keep her balance. Carson had the box in the palm of his two hands.

"We have one more Christmas gift for you, Mom."

Rebecca looked from Carson to Shane to Caleb, and then, with her hand over her pounding heart, her eyes went back to the box, wrapped in gold wrapping paper and topped with a red velvet ribbon.

"*Open it*, Mom." Caleb squirmed excitedly next to Shane.

With trembling fingers, Rebecca took the box from her son's hands. She suddenly found herself in the middle of a marriage proposal, with both of her sons apparently in on the plan. Rebecca slid the red velvet tie off the box before she carefully unwrapped the shiny gold paper to reveal a black box. A jewelry box. A *ring* box.

Shane stepped forward then. "May I?"

She nodded her head and handed him the box. Carson and Caleb crowded around them as Shane opened the box to reveal the present inside. A simple yet elegant engagement ring, with a brilliant-cut white diamond bezel set in rose gold.

"Do you like it?" Caleb asked impatiently.

"Yes." She could barely get the word out.

"Shane asked us if he could marry you," Carson explained.

"And we said *yes*." Her youngest son threw up his arms when he said the word *yes* like he was celebrating a touchdown.

Her mind racing, while her body seemed to be frozen with shock, Rebecca found herself staring into Shane's clear blue eyes while tears of surprise and joy fell onto her cheeks. She quickly wiped them away.

"I can't believe you're going to make me ugly-cry in front of your family."

"Not possible, Rebecca with the pretty eyes." Shane

took the ring out of the box and handed the empty box to his wingman, Carson.

"Rebecca." He took her hand in his. "Ever since I met you, I've made it my mission to become the man who deserved you. If you'll have me, I promise you, I'll make it my mission to love you for the rest of your life."

With her sons as his witnesses, Shane knelt down on one knee and held out the ring as his offering to her.

"Will you marry me, Rebecca?"

No matter how hard she tried not to start crying again, it was hopeless.

"Yes." She nodded, realizing that he did, indeed, get one more yes out of her.

Shane rose, held her hand steady in his and slipped the engagement ring onto her finger. Laughing through her happy tears, Rebecca was the center of a group hug. She kissed her sons on the tops of their heads and then she kissed her fiancé on the lips.

"Dinner's served." Savannah appeared in the doorway, oblivious to the moment that had unfolded between them seconds before. "You'd better hurry. It's going to be a stampede."

Carson and Caleb raced toward the dining room, pretending not to hear Rebecca when she told them not to run. And then she was alone, once again, with the man she loved—the man she was going to marry. Shane held out his arm to her so he could escort her to the formal dining room. As they walked together, Rebecca couldn't stop admiring the sparkling diamond on her left ring finger.

"I can't believe I only got you a watch."

As they passed through the doorway, Shane stopped

beneath a strategically placed cluster of mistletoe. He took her face in his hands, his eyes filled with so much love for her. And just before he kissed her under the Christmas mistletoe, Shane whispered in her ear, "You gave me everything I've ever wanted, my love, the moment you said *yes*."

* * * * *

If you loved this book, be sure to catch up with the rest of The Brands of Montana miniseries:

High Country Cowgirl
A Bride for Liam Brand
A Wedding to Remember
Thankful for You

Available now from Harlequin Special Edition!